Adore

ADDICTED TO YOU #2

K.M. SCOTT

Books by K.M. Scott

If I Dream (Corrupted Love #1)

If You Fight (Corrupted Love #2)

If We Fall (Corrupted Love #3)

Crash Into Me (Heart of Stone #1)

Fall Into Me (Heart of Stone #2)

Give In To Me (Heart of Stone #3)

Heart of Stone Volume One Box Set

Ever After (Heart of Stone #4)

A Heart of Stone Christmas (Heart of Stone #5)

Unforgettable (Heart of Stone #6)

Unbreakable (Heart of Stone #7)

Heart of Stone Volume Two Box Set

Temptation (Club X #1)

Surrender (Club X #2)

Possession (Club X #3)

Satisfaction (Club X #4)

Acceptance (Club X #5)

Crave (Addicted To You #1)

Adore (Addicted To You #2)

Shatter (Addicted To You #3)

Claim (Addicted To You #4)

Books by K.M. Scott writing as Gabrielle Bisset

Blood Avenged (Sons of Navarus #1)

Blood Betrayed (Sons of Navarus #2)

Longing (A Sons of Navarus Short Story)

Blood Spirit (Sons of Navarus #3)

The Deepest Cut (A Sons of Navarus Short Story)

Blood Prophecy (Sons of Navarus #4)

Blood Craving (Sons of Navarus #5)

Blood Eclipse (Sons of Navarus #6)

The Sons of Navarus Box Set #1

The Sons of Navarus Box Set #2

Stolen Destiny (Destined Ones Duology #1)

Destiny Redeemed (Destined Ones Duology #2)

Love's Master

Masquerade

The Victorian Erotic Romance Trilogy

Addiction and obsession brought Ian and Kristina together, and real life tore them apart.

For Ian, Kristina is everything. What began as an obsession has morphed into that something more he so wanted. Kristina is his muse and so much more, but now both of them must make choices that may change everything.

For Kristina, Ian offers all that she's ever wanted. Love. Passion. Adoration. But these come with a price, and the cost of loving him may be more than she's willing to pay.

Adore was previously published as SILK Volume Two.

CHAPTER ONE
Ian

T HE SMOOTH TASTE of vodka washes over my tongue on its way down to where it can do the most damage. Its strength isn't diluted by orange juice or anything else like that. That's for people wanting to enjoy what they're drinking. Enjoying isn't on the menu tonight. Getting fucking blasted so I can't think anymore?

Yeah. That's what I want.

I bothered to get dressed today. That's a change from the past six days. I think somewhere in my mind I mark this day as some kind of ugly anniversary. Seven days since Kristina told me she didn't want to see me anymore.

One week alone without her.

It's been a long week of endless drinking all alone in my apartment. I think I might have eaten a few times in that span. Not that eating is high on my list of priorities. Either is showering, writing, or doing anything that doesn't involve my efforts to forget.

There is no goal other than forgetting, but I know that's futile. I can't forget her. I may say I want to, but that's the last thing I truly want to do. I want to remember every beautiful inch of her body as my hands caressed her silky skin. I want to remember the gentle sound of her voice as she asked me about my work. I want to remember her smile as she lay next to me in bed after we lost ourselves in each other.

I want to remember her. All of her.

I spent the first few days trying to figure out why she doesn't want to see me. What did I do to make her run away? Every time I asked myself that question, my mind came up with the long list of my faults, any one of which could have made her not want me.

You shouldn't have told her about your addictions my brain whispers.

No, she understood. I know she did.

You shouldn't have told her about wanting her before you even met her it murmurs.

No, she's an actress. They understand being desired by fans.

You shouldn't have asked her to be your muse my brain wonders.

No, she loved that. It couldn't be that. She loved it as much as I did.

Lifting the vodka bottle to my lips, I take another gulp and let it slowly trickle down my throat before I set today's companion on the table in front of me. I lean my head back and close my eyes as the alcohol hits my stomach, and for a second the pain eases.

But it doesn't last.

The problem is that I can't turn my brain off. Even with all this vodka in me, my mind can still remember. Like it's on some mission to make sure I don't forget her, it forces me to watch as it replays our time together.

Eyes closed, I can almost feel her on my lap, her thighs spread as she settles onto me. My hands find their place on her hips directing her movement. She looks down at me and gives me one of those sweet smiles that belie how sensual a being she truly is as she rides my cock like no other woman ever has.

"Fuck me, Ian," she whispers lightly against my lips, ratcheting my desire up even higher. I obey. How could I not? Fucking her gives me more than physical release. It lifts my spirit from the darkness that surrounds me to that light and gentle place she provides.

I open my eyes and look around my apartment, disappointed to admit it was just a memory. I grab my phone from the table and scroll through her messages to me. Reading each one, I still can't understand why she left. My fingers hover over the empty space under the last message I sent her. I want to tell her I miss her. That I'm sorry for whatever I did. That I can fix it. Everything can be fixed so it all goes back to the way it was. I can do that.

But they remain frozen hovering over my phone because like every time before when I told myself I should text her, a tiny voice in the back of my mind whispers those dark words and stops me.

Fuck her. She doesn't want to see me? Well, I don't want to fucking see her. She's a Hollywood bitch whose life is a fucking mess. Even her therapist thinks so. For fuck's sake, she thinks she has an addiction to people.

But if she's addicted to people, which in far less stupid terms means she's addicted to their approval and love, how could she leave me?

It always comes back to that question. Every time my mind spins out of control, that voice asks that one question that hurts to even think about because I know addiction. I know the feeling of needing something or someone so fucking bad that your body aches without relief. I know there's no talking yourself out of it if you're addicted.

It's a need, not a want.

So if she has that addiction to people, why didn't she become addicted to me like I did to her?

I clutch my legs as a wave of pain washes over me. My fingernails dig into my thighs just above my knees as the need for her takes me over, and my forearms hurt like someone is twisting them. My muscles ache like someone has placed a heavy object on them, pressing down on me and threatening to crush me with its weight.

I know this feeling. We're old friends. Or enemies, depending on how you view things.

My body craves her. Like the drugs, she got into my system and became part of me. Now that she's gone, every other part of me desperately longs for the missing part.

Maybe if I just text her and ask why she left. Maybe she'll see I care and need her back.

Fuck her. I don't need her. I can live without her.

No, I can't.

I should try to write. Our book waits for me to return to it like some lost orphan who can't understand why its parent abandoned them. Our book. That's the problem. It's not my book. It's ours. Hers and mine. That's why I can't write. She's not here.

Without my muse, I'm lost. Without my Kristina, I can't do it.

Silk will have to wait. Maybe I can find another muse. In whatever stupor I'm in, this sounds like a wonderful idea. Muses can't be that hard to find. Desperate women who want to be adored must be a dime a dozen. Sure. Modern life has made it easy to find them.

Hello, Netflix, my old friend. Show me what you got.

I scroll through the lines of offerings but see little of interest. A blonde would be nice. Kate Silk should have been a blonde the whole time. What was I thinking? Like the world wants another common brown-haired heroine.

Some flick about an outbreak of something catches my eye, and I begin watching it looking for my new muse. I know she's here. My blurry vision isn't helping the search, though. I see a woman, but she's not right. Too trashy. Another enters the scene and she's wrong too. Too sterile.

After about fifteen minutes of what turns out to be a goddamned zombie movie, I go back to the main screen. There's a story in itself—me searching for a muse in a fucking zombie film. Maybe I'll include that in the acknowledgements. *To the hot, half-rotted piece of ass I watched for a quarter of a fucking hour. Literally.* More scrolling through more films I can't imagine anyone thought would be successful brings me to my favorites.

No, I don't need my favorites. I need something new. Someone new.

But the photos from Kristina's films sit there lined up in a row for me to watch. I can't help but chuckle as I think, "Well, I guess we know where Netflix stands on the issue of me and Kristina."

I click on the film that started it all. That remake of The Misfits. I've watched this so many times I could act out the parts myself, but as I sit here in my living room fucked up from too much vodka, I watch it feeling like I'm seeing her for the first time in ages. I wait with eager anticipation for the moment when I know she'll be in the picture. The first time her face appears on the screen, my heart leaps in my chest.

Missing her for the past week has been nothing compared to how I feel as I watch her. I can't go on like this. Every second she's in front of me and I can see her but not touch her or speak to her is killing me.

I need to talk to her. No. Talking is never good, at least not for me. Like most writers, I'm my worst when my mouth is open. No, words come much better from me when they're written. When I have the time to choose the perfect ones to express my thoughts. When I can construct my sentences exactly so she'll understand my true feelings.

Then I'll be able to say the right things.

She always thought I said the perfect words. I remember her saying that.

I reach for my phone and go to her messages again. My thumbs hover over the letters as I think about what I want to say. Jesus, now isn't the time for writer's block. I want to tell her so much. Need to tell her so much. I'm sorry. I don't know what I did, but I'm sorry. Tell me what I did so I can make up for it. Come to me and let me fix this.

None of those words show up on my phone because my fingers never move. After convincing myself I shouldn't do anything, I throw the phone away from me, disgusted. I hate myself for doing nothing.

I can't go on like this.

TEN O'CLOCK ON Wednesday night turns out to be a busy time on the streets of the Upper West Side. Maybe there's some street festival or some event being held, but as the October wind bites at my cheeks, I can't imagine that's the case. Maybe I'm just one of legions of people smashed and needing to see someone, like love zombies who can't do anything but drag their empty selves to where their heart lives. More people out actually works for me tonight, though, since I'm hoping to be invisible.

Not that I'm some huge star or anything like that. I'm no Stephen King or James Patterson, for Christ's sake. It's true I'm a New York Times bestseller, but that doesn't translate into instant notoriety, especially for someone who writes historical fiction. Well, maybe Dan Brown can't walk the streets where he lives without a mob attacking him to take a picture or sign something. My handful of literary successes have allowed me to still be somewhat invisible to most people, however.

I walk the blocks toward her brownstone building slowly and deliberately, mainly because I'm loaded. Every time I take a deep breath and let it out, the smoke from the cold nearly knocks me over from the vodka smell.

The sidewalk is surprisingly uneven now that I'm walking it without her. She always wrapped her arm in mine as we walked. Or maybe it's the effect of the vodka. I don't know. I just know where I'm going.

Her building faces a small patch of grass with a few trees on it. Not really a park, it's more like a front yard of some planned building that never came to fruition. It sits there as a testament to someone's hopes and dreams that never came true. I position myself under one of the trees in the shadows and look up toward the second floor to see her windows darkened.

She isn't there.

Where is she? Why is she out on a Wednesday at just after ten at night?

Before I can stop myself, my mind begins to spiral out of control with scenarios of her out having a good time with someone else. I've spent the entire week since losing her a total fucking mess, and she's out enjoying life. She's probably with someone. Another man. A man who wants her like I do.

No. He can't want her like I do. No one wants her like I do. They merely want to fuck her or watch her act out their stupid parts. I want to watch her sleep next to me. I want to see her smile when I read her the story of us. I want to feel her come apart from my touch. I want her to know I love her more than I can say.

A surge of rage and hate pushes through my body making me want to hit something. My fists ball up at my side as my mind spins with ideas, but then the sinking feeling in my stomach from the reality that she's gone makes me weak.

Stumbling back against the hard trunk of one of the trees, I try to get my emotions under control.

And then I see her. But not just her. I see her step out of a cab with someone. A man. He escorts her up the stairs to the front door while I stand there and watch, my heart in my throat as I wait to see if she kisses him. She's wearing the pink shirt she wore the night we first met at Jax's and a pair of jeans she never wore the entire time we were together. Her long brown hair falls over her shoulders making her even sexier than she could ever know because she has no idea how incredible she looks.

She's smiling at something he must have said. Hate rushes through me again. Not for her, though. If only I could hate her, then this would all be so much simpler.

I don't hate her. I wish it were that easy.

He leans down to kiss her, and it takes every ounce of my willpower to stop me from running across the street to tackle him to the ground and never let him touch her again. Pressing my lips together, I want to close my eyes so I don't see her kiss him, but I can't. It's as if some sadistic force is forcing them open so I must watch.

I know what he's feeling as her lips touch his. He wants more. That's the effect she has. One taste won't be enough. He's thinking he wants her to invite him up to her apartment so he can have more of her. More of those lips on his lips. On his cock.

She pulls away and smiles, but I watch in shock as she enters her building and he walks back down the stairs to the cab I hadn't even noticed was still there. She didn't invite him in.

What does it matter? She's moved on.

BY THE TIME I arrive home, my mind's a mixture of loathing and jealousy that threatens to eat me up. I hate her. I love her. I want to wrap my arms around her and never let her go. I miss her. I crave her touch on my skin so bad I ache.

I fall onto the couch and close my eyes, trying to remember anything other than the sight of her kissing that man. My mind begins to race through every moment with her. I struggle to focus on any one time, desperate for one memory that doesn't seem tainted by what I just saw.

My heart slams against my chest and cold sweat pours down over my face. I miss her so much. But then slowly, the images in my mind begin to fade away until one memory comes into focus.

Kristina smiles at me as she takes my finger in her mouth to taste the sugar left on my fingertip. She looks adorable sucking the sweetness from my skin.

"Taste good?" I ask as I slide my finger from her mouth.

Her answer is to kiss me gently on the lips before she runs her tongue over her bottom lip and whispers, "I'd rather have something else to suck on."

I know that might not be entirely true. She's only sucked me off twice before, and while each time she seemed enthusiastic, I know she's never finished anyone else off but me.

"First we taste this martini I made you. Then we can figure out what you should do with that pretty mouth of yours."

Handing her the sugar-rimmed glass, I watch her take a sip of the caramel appletini we've spent the last half hour concocting. The drink only took about ten minutes. The rest of the time would be considered more foreplay than drink making.

That's how it is with her. I know she might be considered needy by some men, but I adore that neediness that would turn others off. I understand it. When I look into her blue eyes and see what can only be described as a craving to be touched or kissed, I know how she feels.

I feel it too.

"It's very sweet, Ian," she says, smacking her lips.

"Then it's perfect for you."

Kristina places her drink on the counter and nuzzles my neck, sending strings of excitement racing through my body. "Maybe I want something less *sweet."*

"I can do less sweet too," I say and tug hard on her hair, pulling her head back so she has to look at me. I look down into those cornflower blue eyes staring up at me with such need. "I can definitely do less sweet."

Biting her lip, she moans softly. "Yes. Please."

What she wants is to be dominated. Not with whips, chains, or any of that other bullshit that's more props than anything else. No, what she wants is me to make her body surrender like no other man has.

I pull her hair harder into my grip, and she doesn't wince in pain so much as in pleasure. A tiny moan escapes from her lips, making my cock swell. I want to conquer her, to make her mine and only mine.

My hand roughly slides down to between her legs and I thrust two fingers into her already dripping pussy. Her eyes grow wide at the invasion, and I ask, "Whose is this?"

"Yours," she says in the sweetest voice I've ever heard.

"Say my name," I order. "Whose is this?"

"Ian's."

I slowly slide my fingers out of her only to ram them back into her warm and willing body. She wants it rougher, but not yet. Eventually.

"Fucking right." I unzip my pants and take out

my rock hard cock. She glances down toward it and bites her lip again. "And whose cock is the only one you want?"

Tentatively, she reaches out to touch me, stroking me from base to head. "Yours. I mean, Ian's."

I tighten my hold in her hair. "If you can't remember my name, I think it's time for you to learn it."

Her eyes widen because she knows what's coming next. I tear off her skirt and blouse, sending buttons flying everywhere around my kitchen, before I push her up against the wall. Her face wild with excitement, she whimpers as I lift her and command her to wrap her legs around my waist, and then I slam into that wet cunt that's only mine and fuck her harder than I ever imagined she could handle.

She takes every pound, every slam into her body and begs for more. I sink my teeth into her shoulder, and she cries out but doesn't plead for me to stop. I know her legs ache from clutching me. I know she must want to stop, but she doesn't. Not until she gives me what I want. Not until I give her what she wants.

I feel her body begin to contract around my cock, surrendering to all the pain and pleasure I've given her. She whimpers, "Ian, don't stop...harder...harder..."

I thrust my hips forward once more and bury myself in her as deep as I can as she clings to me more *with every moment. Her release rushes through her and sends me over the edge, and I flood her body with all I have. I have no idea how long we stay there like that, our bodies trembling against one another and our breathing heavy and sated.*

She's small and broken afterward, but she's mine to cradle and whisper tender words to. I carry her to the bed and hold her until all the pain eases away and all that's left are the most exquisite moments between two people who need each other. My hands, which had inflicted so much on her as we fucked, now gently stroke her skin in love. She entwines her fingers in mine and curls our hands together under her chin as I tell her how much I adore her and mean every word as if my life depended on their truth. I listen to her breathing as she drifts off to sleep, and just before I close my eyes, I hear her sigh contentedly.

I've never been happier with another soul in my life.

I open my eyes as the reality of my lonely rooms bears down on me. I don't know how to go on feeling like this. I don't want to go on feeling like this. I need something to help me not feel at all.

CHAPTER TWO

Kristina

I SIT IN front of my makeup mirror hating what stares back at me. Lines and wrinkles already and I'm only in my twenties. I use the finest creams and lotions. Why don't they work on me? My skin looks ruddy and uncared for.

My eyes, all red-rimmed and watery looking, tell the story of who I've become in the past week. I cry all the time when I'm alone, which is far too often. I cry when I read those texts I sent him. I cry when I see the texts he's sent me. I cry that he hasn't sent me any more.

I'm a mess. A stereotypical Hollywood mess, complete with bad skin and red eyes.

I think back to my lunch with Cilla that day when all she could talk about was how I glowed. Now that's gone and all I am is the miserable wretch that stares back at me as I try to cover her up with makeup.

Magazines I've appeared in sit stacked on a

table next to me, but no matter how many times I thumb through their glossy pages, the compliments don't feel real. Gorgeous eyes. Beautiful smile. Healthy skin. They all rave about my look, but it's all lies.

I'm all lies.

I ran away from Ian because he scared me, but I've been miserable without him since. I thought I saw him last night, but the more I think about it, the more I know that was all in my mind. It seemed so real, though. I was on my front stairs with Gavin, a fellow actor I hope to work with in that film I screen tested for, and as he leaned in to kiss me goodnight, I thought I caught a glimpse of Ian standing in the trees across the street.

Stop doing this! You're a Hollywood star, Kristina Richards! You can meet another man—hundreds of them, if you want, anytime you want.

I say this every time I feel down and want to go back to Ian, and it works. For a few minutes anyway. Sometimes if I'm busy during the day or I go out and see lots of men looking at me, it works for a few hours. But eventually, the truth comes back and I'm alone in my apartment missing him so much it hurts.

There's not enough concealer to hide my dark circles and bags now. I put more on, but that only makes it worse. Frustrated, I throw it aside and move on to creating the face the world expects. Foundation for even, glowing skin that's having a hard time finding its glow lately. Grey eyeliner and jet black mascara for smoky eyes that cry more than seduce these days. Grey eye shadow to complete that look.

I throw the shadow brush down onto my makeup table and bury my face in my hands. No matter how much I apply, it can't change the truth. My miserable inside shows all over my outside. Tears flow down my cheeks, and I don't stop them. I can't. It's like I have an inexhaustible supply of them.

All I can think of is him. What's he doing now? Is he finished with our book? Is it even our book to him anymore? I can't help but cry harder at the thought that it's not our book anymore. I was his muse. He adored me and wanted to write because of me.

And what did I do? I ran away.

But he scared me. I know that scene he wrote with his character was actually about him. He was watching me.

As soon as the words form in my head, my brain discounts them as nonsense.

He adored you, and you ran away like a child who couldn't handle being watched. Millions of people watch you every day. Do you run away from being an actress to become a sheep herder hidden away on some farm? No! So why did you run away from him?

Shaking my head, I answer my own question as I try to push those thoughts away. I don't know why. I was scared. Now all I feel is lonely without him.

But if he loved me so much, why hasn't he come back? Why hasn't he tried to contact me since that night? There have been no flowers, no calls, no texts. No anything.

I lower my hands to see the mess my face has become from my tears and makeup mixing together. *This is why you're alone. You're not beautiful, no matter how many magazines say so. They lie. Everyone lies when they say you're beautiful and gorgeous because if you were, Ian would have come by now.*

No! I can't let those demons in me do this every time I look in the mirror. I grab a tissue and clean the mascara from under my eyes, but it's no use. I can't do this. No matter how much makeup I put on my face, it will never hide how unhappy I am.

A HAND WAVES from the back of the very dark bar, and I squint my eyes to see whose it is. My friend Sienna stands from her seat and calls my name, so I begin to make my way through the crowds of smiling and laughing people who all look happier than I feel. I reach her and see she's found us a table far enough away from the front of the bar that we'll have at least a little privacy.

She's in a black dress that makes her long blond hair stand out more than usual, and I see by the number of men around her that it will be the usual when we're out. A line of potential second husbands stretching out the door to meet her. Not that I blame them. Between a knockout body and a gorgeous face, she physically has it all going for her. Add to those intelligence and a wickedly sharp sense of humor, and Sienna's the whole package.

"Kristina, I thought we said nine. It's quarter to ten. I'm already half in the bag from waiting here, not to mention the half dozen or so men I've had to brush off because it's a girls' night out."

"I'm sorry," I say as I sit down with my back to the crowd. "It took me longer than usual to get my makeup right."

She narrows her eyes to a judgmental squint and studies my face. "Have you been drinking already?"

I shake my head. "No. Why?"

"Your eyes are all glassy looking. What are

you doing?"

Instantly more self-conscious than when I walked in the door, I lower my head. "Nothing. Nothing at all."

"Did your makeup artist friend give you something again? I told you not to trust her. That woman is bad news."

"No. Nothing."

Sadie, the woman who's been the makeup artist on my last two films, isn't the type of person Sienna would ever spend any real time with. She's not the right class, in her mind. It also doesn't help that she gave me some pills one time to help me with insomnia that was crippling me and making it impossible to work. They made me a little crazy for a few days, but in Sienna's eyes, it was intentional.

"Then what's up with you? Cilla gave me chapter and verse about whatever regimen you've begun using and how you were glowing like a goddamned nuclear reactor. No offense, but either she's blind or the effects have worn off."

I rub my fingertips over my cheek as if to feel if the evidence of my misery is written all over my face. "You know how she is. It's always something to rave about with her."

The waiter arrives just in time to save me from more of this interrogation, and I order a merlot. Tonight's definitely a merlot night. No sweet and fruity red wines for me. If I'm going to look like shit, I might as well get shitfaced.

Sienna gives my wrist a squeeze and launches back into her questioning. "So who is this mystery man you've begun to see lately? Cilla couldn't talk about much of anything else, except your glowing, of course. I want details."

"Wouldn't you rather tell me all about your new movie? I mean, this is looking like it's going to be the one," I say, hoping to use her inherent actor's ego to my advantage, but she isn't having any of it. Unlike Cilla, Sienna knows when bullshit is being thrown her way. It's one of the reasons I consider her such a dear friend.

"Kristina, what's going on here? You look like shit, show up nearly an hour late, and now you don't want to tell me about this guy. You can tell me. This is Sienna you're talking to, not some stranger. We've talked each other through all the ups and downs. Well, talked and drank, which is perfect since we're in a bar. I promise to keep the alcohol flowing if you promise to talk. You look like you need it."

I want so much to tell someone about Ian and how much I miss him. I'm not even afraid of turning into a sobbing mess in public. At least I'd be able to unburden myself of my misery. But I can't because I promised him I wouldn't tell anyone about us and I keep my promises.

Even if there isn't an us anymore.

"We aren't seeing each other now. It's over."

Sienna's expression tells me how awful I must look. Her deep brown eyes fill with pity, and she gives my wrist another squeeze, this time one of those empathetic "I'm here for you" squeezes. "What happened?"

"I really don't want to talk about it, Sienna. It's just over. I feel terrible about it, though, so if this girls' night can help me forget, I'd really appreciate it."

"Got it!" she says with loads of enthusiasm as she raises her hand to get the attention of the waiter. "We're going to need something more than wine then."

The man returns to our table and she instructs him to bring over a bottle of his finest cognac. Never a huge fan of brandy, I grimace at the thought of a cognac hangover. As he walks away, I lean toward her and say, "I'm not really a big cognac drinker, Sienna."

"Honey, the cognac isn't to drink so much as to advertise for a certain kind of man. Look around this bar. You've got beer drinkers, who you can do better than; wine drinkers, who aren't really what I think would help you forget anyone;

and liquor drinkers. Within that last group are men who understand that if a woman can afford to drink the finest cognac in the house, then she's expecting a certain level of man. That's the man I'm trying to find for you tonight."

The thought of going with anyone other than Ian fills me with dread. I try to pretend that I'm all for her plan, but inside I wish I was back in my apartment on my couch reading his book instead of sitting in a bar full of men Sienna planned on having audition for the role of my next boyfriend.

"I'm not ready to meet anyone new yet," I say as the bottle of cognac arrives at our table.

Sienna pours each of us a drink and lifts her glass to make a toast. "I'm not talking about starting some long term relationship, Kristina. Tonight's about finding someone to give you a good lay and make you forget the mystery man. To great sex and its healing powers!"

I clink my glass and lift it to my lips to take a drink. I have to admit it does taste nice. Maybe I've only had cheaper cognac before.

Her plan works almost instantly, and within a few minutes men begin to surround our table, each one dying to join us at what's obviously a celebration. If they only knew how depressed I truly am, they'd be running away instead of doing their best to win us. I smile and laugh at their jokes, but I can't help but notice that most of them are far more interested in Sienna than in me.

Not that this is a bad thing. The idea to drink and then fuck Ian out of my mind was never going to work, no matter how I tried. Sienna may not believe it, but I know the truth. I love him and nothing and no one else could change that. Love isn't something that can just be replaced.

"My name is Brian. What's yours?" a voice says, tearing me out of my fog of thinking about where I really want to be at that moment.

I look at the man seated next to me and smile. Attractive with wavy brown hair and brown eyes, he looks like a banker or businessman in his expensive grey pinstriped suit. "I'm Kristina. It's nice to meet you, Brian."

"You look out of place here, Kristina. By that I mean, you don't look like you want to be here."

So perfect strangers can see it too.

"No, I'm having a good time. My friend and I are out for a girls' night out." Looking across the table, I see Sienna has a man on each side of her, both working hard for her attention.

"It just seems your heart isn't in this," he says with a gentle smile that shows his very white teeth.

"I'm not as good at it as Sienna, I think. Some

people shine in crowds. Others are less comfortable and prefer one-on-one."

I take a drink of my wine and feel a rush of heat cross my cheeks as I realize I've just intimated I want to be alone with him. I don't, but at that moment as the merlot settles into me, I don't want to be alone. He might not be the man I want, but at least he's someone who likes me.

"Would you like another drink?"

My wine glass is almost empty, so I nod. "That would be nice. Thank you."

Brian raises his arm to get the server's attention and then turns his attention back to me. "Kristina, what do you do for a living?"

"I'm an actress." I don't say it, but I can't help thinking I'm not a very successful one since I'm able to sit in a bar with hundreds of people around and not be noticed, however.

He nods and pretends to be interested, but I see in his eyes a look of disappointment as he explains his job as a day trader. I listen intently for any sign that he has the passion I love to find in people, but Brian is a businessman through and through. There's nothing really wrong with that, but I like my men to be more intense and creative.

Like Ian.

We continue to talk, each of us pretending

there's anything interesting about the other person beyond looks, but Sienna's plan has failed. Looking across the table, I see that's only partially true. I might not have met anyone I have any interest in, but by the look on her face, she's definitely interested in the blond man sitting close to her.

At least one of us will be happy tonight.

I look at Brian and say, "I think I'm going to head home. It was very nice to meet you." Stretching my hand across the table, I tap on Sienna's arm to get her attention. "I'm going home. I'm just going to catch a cab, so don't worry about me. Talk to you later."

"Are you sure? There's more cognac. We can move to the other side of the bar, if you like." Sienna's not-so-subtle way of asking if I'm leaving because I dislike Brian makes me laugh, and after rolling my eyes toward him to hopefully show him I'm not leaving because of him, I shake my head.

"I think it's just an early night for me. Enjoy yourself."

I turn to say goodbye to Brian, but he's standing now and I sense he's looking to take our conversation outside. Why I can't imagine since neither one of us set anything on fire with our discussion of how exciting we think our jobs are.

Sienna gives me a look as if to say, "Is it okay he's going?" but I just nod and smile. Some company as I wait for a cab won't be a horrible thing, even if it's just someone silently standing next to me.

Of course, the minute I get outside it seems that every cab in the city has disappeared suddenly. I look up and down the street over and over, but nothing. It's like fate is forcing me to move on, even though I don't want to.

"I can give you a ride, if you like. My company has a car service we use, so I can have it drop you off anywhere you like."

I stop my head swiveling left and right and say, "That's really nice of you. I'm just going to take a cab, I think. But thank you."

"There's not a cab in sight. Let me get you a car and I can take you right to your apartment."

I look once more up and down the block and sigh. I know I shouldn't do it, but I have no other way home and my apartment is miles away from this bar in Brooklyn. With a sigh, I relent and say, "Okay. Thanks."

Brian calls the car service and then says, "If you're nervous, I can stay here and not join you. I don't want you to think I'm some kind of creepy stalker guy. I'm just a nice guy trying to help someone get home."

Hanging my head, I say quietly, "Thank you. I'm not really a miserable person. Really. I've just been through something recently and my friend wanted to show me a good time. The odds were pretty much stacked against her with that, though."

"I don't think you're miserable. You seem nice. Nothing like what I imagined an actress would be like. You're down-to-earth. I like that."

I thank him for the compliment and we talk for a while about the weather, our careers again, and other noncommittal, superficial topics until a black town car pulls up. As I climb into the backseat, he stands at the door waiting for me to say whether he can join me or not. I can't be a total bitch, so waving him in, I say, "Please join me. It's the least I can do since you got me a ride home."

Brian and I talk the whole way to the Upper West Side, and in some way, I realize I do like him. Not in any romantic way, but as a person, he seems nice. That doesn't mean I trust him, though, so instead of telling the driver my address, I tell him Ian's. I'll just get out there and after the car drives away, I'll make my way home.

The car pulls up to the entrance of Ian's building and I turn toward Brian. "Thank you. This was very nice of you."

Smiling, he leans in and kisses me. I don't know if it should make me feel something for him, but all I feel is how much I miss Ian. I kiss him back and quickly get out of the car. He's probably disappointed I didn't ask for his number or give him mine, but I don't care.

The car speeds down the street away from Ian's building, and I know I should just turn away and walk home, but I can't. I know he's up there right now. This was a mistake. I shouldn't have gotten out here. Now all I want to do is see him.

The doorman recognizes me and gives me a big smile. "Good evening, Miss Richards! It's nice to see you again."

I smile meekly, knowing what I'm about to do is a mistake. Walking toward the door, I wish him a good evening as he lets me into the building, thrilled to know Ian never told him not to, and my heart begins to beat wildly. I should just turn around and go home, but he's just a few floors up. I can't stop myself.

Pressing the button for the elevator, I tell myself this is a mistake. He's never texted or called back after telling me we'd see each other again. What if he's changed his mind? What if he's found someone else to be his muse?

My heart sinks at the thought of him writing because of another woman. Being his muse had made me special. If he'd replaced me…

The elevator dings to let me know I'm at his floor and as I step out into the hallway leading to his apartment, fear grips me making it nearly impossible to walk toward his door. I can see it, that familiar entrance to his home I've walked through so many times before, but now it just looks like a black void.

Like what lies behind it isn't somewhere I'm welcome anymore.

With every step, my fear grows until I reach the end of the hallway and hear noises from inside his apartment. Is he watching television? I lift my hand to knock, but a sound stops me dead. Placing my ear next to the door, I listen and hear a moan.

A woman's moan.

I can't move from that spot, yet that's all I want to do. I desperately want to run away and never come back here again. Unable to leave, I can't help but cry. He's in there with another woman. Another muse. I've been replaced.

Like some pitiful, unwanted animal, I stay there on his doorstep as the sounds of him with someone else fill my ears. Finally, they become too much and I can't stand it anymore. Running away, I stumble to the elevator as my tears blind me and I press the buttons to get me out of there before he sees me and knows how pathetic I truly am.

CHAPTER THREE

Ian

I OPEN THE door just as the last sight of Kristina disappears into the elevator. For a moment, I consider running after her, but I stop myself. I'm half-naked standing in my doorway after fucking a woman I picked up in a bar. This isn't exactly the way I want the woman I love to see me.

Jessica, or whatever her name is, wants to cuddle like we're some romantic couple, but I quickly send her on her way with a smile and an empty promise that we have to do this again sometime. I needed her to help me forget Kristina. She didn't do the job, but that's not her fault.

Grabbing my phone, I type out a text and even though I know she heard me fucking someone else, I hope she'll read it.

Kristina, I miss you. Why did you run away when I opened the door?

Not exactly my best prose, but texting isn't my medium.

I sit and wait for her to answer as I fantasize about when we finally will see each other again. I want to look into those beautiful cornflower blue eyes and see that she missed me like I missed her. I can't wait to feel her lips touch mine in a kiss that makes us both forget whatever it was that broke us up. My body hurts I want her so badly, and only she can ease this ache inside.

My phone vibrates across the top of the table, and my heart slams against my chest as I anticipate her answer. Hands shaking, I pick it up and begin to read, knowing immediately that she's just as moving in text as she is in person.

> *How could you forget me so quickly? Wasn't I your muse? You've already replaced me. How could you do that?*

The palpable hurt in her words makes me feel like someone's stabbing me in the chest. I don't know why she left, but this isn't the message of a woman who doesn't want to see a man.

Her texts continue to come as she pours her heart out to me.

> *Didn't what we were to each other mean anything to you?*
> *I thought when you told me you couldn't think*

*of anyone else that you meant it. I heard you
with her when I came to your door.*

My fingers twitch as I think about what to type back to her. This isn't my best way of communicating, so whatever I say will probably come out all fucked up. Better for me to just listen.

A few minutes later, a much longer message comes in and she breaks my heart with just a few words.

I can't bear the silence from your end. Are you getting these messages? Don't you care that I miss you? Please say something. I can't go on like this. Do you miss me like I miss you? I lie in bed at night thinking about you and wishing you'd call, but you never do. Why?

As much as I know I should message her back and tell her how I feel—how I miss her more than I can even describe and how I feel like part of my body's been ripped away without her in my life—I don't. Maybe I want the chance to say what's in my heart in person. Maybe I don't know what to say.

Or maybe I'm punishing her in some tiny way for leaving me.

Whatever the reason, I don't answer her. Instead, for the first time in over a week, I want to write. Turning my laptop on, I wait for it to warm up as a hundred ideas for Silk race through my mind. The creative floodgates open, and I can barely keep up with all that I want to write. By the time my fingers hit the keyboard for the first time since she left, it's like they're on fire.

I type like a madman, words flowing through my hands like never before. I'm inspired by Kristina again. My muse has returned. A week ago, my creativity had dried up, gone with the woman I adored, but now I can see the end of the book. All those nights of missing her and being awash in alcohol are past now.

My writing comes out in ways that are entirely new to me. Always a very deliberate author, I'm now a man on a mission. Our book must be completed.

Nearly two hours later, I sit back and look at what Kristina's return to my life has brought to me. The first draft of Silk is finished. I've never been prouder of any creative effort in my life, and I know it's all due to her.

I take a shower, shave for the first time in eight days, and dress in clothes I know she'll love. Now to convince her to see me after what I did earlier. Seated back on my couch, I type the best words I have and hope they'll be enough.

Come to me. I miss you and need you. I was

lost without you.

She doesn't answer. I wait ten minutes. Then twenty minutes. Finally, at thirty minutes I begin to think I might never see her again.

No. I told her we'd see each other again, and we will. I don't know how and I don't know when, but we will.

I'll make sure of that.

A knock on my front door stirs me from my thoughts, and I walk toward it knowing it's her even before I look through the peephole. I feel her close to me again. It's like a fire inside my chest that burns only for her.

I open it slowly, barely containing my impatience to have her by my side again. She's standing there, her eyes wide and filled with insecurity. I don't blame her. How could I? The last time she stood in that very spot she heard me fucking another woman.

"Please don't send me away again," she says quietly in a plaintive voice that makes me want her even more.

"I never sent you away."

She steps into my arms and in one long moment everything I've ever wanted is mine again. Her body melds to mine like a missing part finally returned. Standing there in my doorway, I hold her and I'm happy.

I feel her sob against my chest and squeeze my arms around her to bring her closer. I want to crawl inside her so she can never leave me again. She sweetly fingers the buttons on my shirt and asks, "Is she still here?"

"No. She was nothing, Kristina."

She looks up at me with hurt-filled eyes. "Then why did you go with her?"

"I tried to forget you, so I went to a bar and picked someone up. I thought maybe being with someone else would work, but all it did was make me miss you more. Then when you came to the door before, I had sense you were there so I went to the door looking for you."

"I heard you with her."

I don't know what to say to this, so I pull her into the apartment and close the door. Wrapping my arms around her, I whisper against the top of her head, "I'm sorry. Forgive me."

"I wanted to die when I heard those sounds coming from in here."

Tilting her head up so she has to look at me, I kiss her gently on the lips. "You have to forgive me, Kristina. Tell me you can."

She hangs her head. "I want to say no, to tell you I can never forgive you, Ian." She stops and stays silent for so long that I wonder if she truly can't forgive me. Then she speaks, and my world is right again. "I can't, though. I just can't."

I lift her chin with my finger and look down into that beautiful face looking up at me. "Forgive me and know I'll never touch another woman."

"Never?" she asks, not believing me.

"Never. How could I want anyone but my muse?"

She smiles and I know she'll forgive me.

I kiss her forehead and pull back to ask her a much harder question. Looking into her eyes, I look for the truth as I ask, "Why did you run away from me?"

Her smile fades into a deep frown. "You frightened me."

"How?" A surge of anger, not at her but at myself, rushes through me at the thought that anything I did made her frightened.

"When you wrote that scene about Kate standing outside the house of the man she loves. She was stalking him, and I thought you wrote that because you did that to me. I know you would never hurt me, but it scared me. So I ran away."

Backing up, I release her, now angry with her too. "I did do that. Just like the character, I stood outside your apartment one night and watched just to see you. But that you think me doing that would harm you makes me wonder if you know me at all, Kristina."

She reaches out to touch me, but I won't let her. The frustration and fear of losing me again registers in her expression. When she speaks, it's even clearer. "Ian, don't say that. I know you. Don't say I don't."

"You say you know me, but you think I'd hurt you? You think missing you so much that I stand out on the sidewalk across the street from your building praying for just a glimpse of you is me wanting to hurt you?"

I back up even further from her and watch the tears well in her eyes. This reunion isn't turning out how I'd hoped it would, but I can't change who I am and she deserves to know that.

Kristina grabs my hand and holds it tight. "I'm sorry. I've spent so much time worrying about stalkers. I didn't mean that I was afraid you'd hurt me, though. Tell me you know that. Please tell me you know that."

I try to pull my hand away, but she refuses to let go and I pull her into me. For a long moment, we stare at each other afraid of what the next words may be from the other's mouth. I can't do anything but admit who I am again and remind her of the kind of man she's with.

"I'm addicted to you. I have been since the first time I saw you, days before meeting you that first night. It's who I am. I became addicted to how you make me feel, and that night I stood outside looking up at your windows, I wanted to feel that. I can't change this, Kristina."

"You're addicted to me like a drug?" she asks in a confused voice.

I nod. "Just like a drug. When I'm with you, I feel like the man I want to be but most times can't be. But with you, I can. When I'm not with you, I crave your touch, the taste of your lips, the sound of your voice, your smile when I read what I've written to you. Most of the time, I'm okay just knowing I'll see you again, but other times…"

My voice trails off as I remember how I felt standing outside her apartment staring up at her windows. "Other times, like that night, I want so much to see you that I'd willingly hide in the shadows just for a glimpse of you from the street below."

My confession doesn't frighten her, but I see in her eyes her confusion. Her therapist was wrong. She doesn't get addicted to people. If she did, she'd know exactly what this feels like.

"I missed you so much. I couldn't eat. I couldn't sleep. I couldn't do anything. I'm sorry I got scared. I was being stupid."

I kiss her lips and cradle her face. "You weren't stupid. I never thought that would frighten you, but you weren't stupid."

She's quiet for a moment, and then the question she asks me makes me more jealous than I ever thought possible. "What if I slept with someone else too?"

All at once, I want to push her away and hold her to me. I bite out, "Did you?"

"No, but I can tell it bothers you. Now you know how I feel."

I drop my hands from her face and walk away from her. "Feelings aren't like that. I can't know what you feel any more than you can know what I feel, other than if we tell each other."

"Then let me tell you how I feel. Like my heart was being ripped from my chest. I heard you in here with her. Heard her making the same sounds I make when you make love to me. I wanted to run away but all I could do was stand there and listen to you with her. That's how I feel, Ian!"

I turn around to face her. "You said you forgave me."

"I did, but that doesn't mean it doesn't still hurt to think about it. Maybe I should go out and fuck another man. I could have tonight. I met someone at a bar and he gave me a ride here. I could call him and then maybe you'd know how I feel."

"Don't."

"Don't what? Make you understand what it feels like when you know the person you care about is with someone else? Imagine yourself outside my apartment door hearing me moan another man's name as he fucks me. I'm on his lap straddling his hips riding his cock and I make that noise you love—the one like a whimper right before I come. Imagine hearing that, Ian. And then I want you to just forgive me."

Her anger isn't just at me. I know that. But it doesn't change how much her words fucking hurt. I hate the man she met tonight. I don't care that she didn't do anything with him. I hate him.

And I love her.

I walk to her and can't hold back. I want her. I need her. "Not another fucking word, Kristina. You're mine. No one else. Do you understand?"

"No, I don't," she sobs. "I don't understand how to forget you with her, Ian. Make me understand."

Stuffing my hands into her hair, I pull her head back and kiss her hard. Her mouth surrenders to mine and as I snake my tongue past her lips to tease hers, an ache in my hard cock spreads throughout my body.

"I need you so fucking bad," I whisper against her lips. "I never needed her like you. I never wanted her like you."

Kristina's hands slide down my chest to unbutton my pants, her fingers fumbling with the zipper as we kiss. Finally, she slides her hand beneath my boxer briefs and palms my cock, and it stiffens even more. "Tell me what you did with her."

"No," I groan as she slowly strokes my cock.

"Then I'll assume you did the same things with her and won't do them again. Tell me."

I tug her hair harder and close my eyes as she rubs the head of my cock. "I took her from behind. I could pretend it was you if I didn't see her face."

Kristina kisses me as she plays with my cock and then says, "Then you can't do that with me just like you won't let me use my fingers with you."

I want her so bad at that moment, I agree. "Deal. Now get those clothes off unless you want them to end up ripped off your body."

She slides her skirt down her legs to reveal nothing underneath. Her pussy, clean shaven and bare, makes me want to bury my face in her, and as she strips off her sweater, I drop to my knees to taste her. With my thumbs, I open her folds so no part of her is hidden to me and gently flick my tongue up her gorgeous wet slit, loving her taste on my tongue. Musky and sweet, she's all I want in my mouth.

Her hands tighten in my hair when my tongue reaches her clit, and I suck it into my mouth, knowing what it will do to her. Above me, she moans my name and my cock twitches its need to be inside her.

I stand and kiss her, letting her taste her own juices. "That's what I crave when you're not here. The taste of that pretty cunt on my tongue."

Biting her lip, she leads me toward the windows. I know what she wants. She wants to show the world as much as she's mine, I'm hers. I step out of the rest of my clothes and pull her body to me. "Not feeling so shy anymore?"

She shakes her head and smiles not-so-innocently. "Not tonight. I want everyone to see us."

I wrap my arm around her waist and pull her to me. "Come here. I want you on your knees sucking my cock."

Slowly, she lowers herself to the floor and opens her mouth. I guide my cock between her lips and thrust hard so the head butts up against the back of her throat. I want to fuck her face like I want to fuck her cunt.

Hard and deep.

Her hand wraps around the base, giving her

some control, but I push my hands into her hair and grip tightly to direct her as she sucks me. I love the feel of her mouth and tongue gliding over my skin while she looks up at me with those gentle eyes as I ram my cock into her.

I want to claim her. I want anyone who sees her to know that mouth is only for me. I want my cum to mark her as mine.

It doesn't take long for just the sight of her sucking me off to get me there, and I gently slide my fingertips over her jaw as a sign that I'm about to come. She knows and doesn't stop, taking all of me into her mouth as I shoot down her throat. Eyes closed, she continues to suck as I empty my balls into her.

Sitting back on her heels, she licks her lips and smiles up at me. "I'm getting better at that, don't you think?"

I tilt her chin up toward me. "What does my Kristina want?"

"You. I want you inside me."

I lower myself to the floor and pushing her hair off her face, kiss her long and deep. I love her. I want her. But even more than that, I need her. Only she can make me happy. I trace the outline of her beautiful lower lip with the pad of my thumb, and she takes it into her mouth, sucking the tip so erotically my cock strains against my body in need.

As she looks up at me with those blue eyes so sweet, I say in a low voice, "I want you from behind." I know what I said before, but I can't allow anything to come between us.

"Ian…" she says, pleading for me to do as she asked earlier.

"I want us to share everything. Nothing can stand between us."

CHAPTER FOUR

Kristina

"BUT YOU DID that—"

"We'll never get past that if it's always between us. Give me this, and I'll give you anything your heart desires, Kristina."

I close my eyes and think about how I felt as I stood outside his door listening to him with her. He's right. I'll never be able to forget that if it remains between us.

But my stomach turns at the idea of being with him like that now.

Slowly, I shake my head. I can't do it.

"Open your eyes and look at me, Kristina."

His words aren't a request, but I don't want to look at him. He's pushing too hard, and a tiny part inside me wants to run away again. "No."

"Don't do this. Don't shut me out. Give me what I asked and everything I am is yours."

His words sound strained, as if my refusal hurts him. Slowly, I open my eyes and see the pain in his gaze as he watches me. "I'm scared, Ian. Scared you're going to ask for this tonight and then leave me tomorrow. Scared I don't mean as much to you as you do to me."

"You're everything to me, Kristina. Every fucking thing. I spent every day here missing you so much it hurt. My body ached without you. I couldn't think about anything else. I couldn't write. I couldn't do anything without you. Baby, I need you so much I'm lost."

I hang my head to hide my tears I can't hold back anymore. "It hurts so much to know that you were with her. But like you said, you can't know how that feels because you aren't feeling it. Maybe I should go."

"And do what? Run away again?"

His words edge with sharpness, and I look up to see anger in his face. I don't deserve that anger, but if he wanted to feel it, then I'd hurt him too.

"No. If I leave, I'm going to find someone else to fuck tonight. Then you'll know how much it hurts, Ian."

"I told you don't say that," he whispers, his voice bristling with rage.

"Don't say I want you to understand how much you hurt me?"

He slides his hands into my hair and tugs roughly before he whispers against my lips,

"Don't talk about you with someone else."

"Not just with someone else, Ian. Imagine knowing I was going down on another man, sucking his cock dry like I do with you. Imagine knowing what you thought was so special is nothing but something so common I could find it with someone I meet in a bar."

His fingers tremble with anger against my head, but I know I'm getting through to him. I want him to feel what I felt, so I say the words I know will seal the pain into him. "Imagine another man getting me off and feeling like I'm his, Ian."

The hurt radiates off him. His eyes narrow and he winces as the meaning of my words sink into his mind. I don't know if I should be afraid, but I'm governed by pain so much that I can't stop.

"Does that hurt?"

When he finally speaks, his words are carefully measured but I know I've succeeded. "Kristina, I want to put this behind us. You left me. What I did with that woman meant nothing to me, but you with someone else would mean a great deal to me."

"How much?"

"How much what?" he asks as he presses his body tightly to mine.

"How much would me fucking another man mean to you, Ian?" When he doesn't answer, I ask the question again, louder this time. "How much would it mean to you if I fucked another man, Ian?"

I see something flash in his eyes, and he stands me up and spins me around to face the window and the outside world I so wanted to see me claim him just a few minutes ago. With his palm pressed against my throat, he whispers low and deep in my ear, "You want to hear me say I hate the idea of you with someone else, Kristina? That I'd want to kill him if I knew you'd been with him? That just the thought of it makes my fucking chest hurt like someone's carving into me? Is that what you want?"

Staring at the reflection of him standing behind me, I see the agony in his eyes as he speaks those words, and I answer truthfully. "Yes."

He slides his hand between my legs and thrusts two fingers inside me, making my legs go weak when he adds the pad of his thumb to press on my clit. "Then hear me now. You're mine. Only I get to be inside you. Only I get to taste your body. And yes, I would kill him if I found out you'd been with another man."

I can't help but moan as he speaks and his fingers fuck me. But can I let him be with me like he was with her?

"I don't want to hear another thing about anyone else, Kristina. Do you understand? There is no one else for me, and there is no one else for you. Now put your hands against the window and brace yourself."

The thought of protesting—of saying no—passes through my mind, but before I have the chance to say anything, he's so deep inside me I feel like I can't breathe. I push my damp palms against the glass, feeling its smooth surface slide under my touch, but his hands on my hips hold me fast to him, making sure I don't fall.

Each thrust into me pushes my body forward, and each time he leaves me I fall back, my body searching for what only he can give me. His fingers press hard into the flesh covering my hipbones, but whatever pain I feel is masked by the pleasure his cock sliding in and out of me provides.

His lips skim my neck and he says low in my ear, "I missed you so fucking much, Kristina. I couldn't do anything but think of you and hope the pain of being without you went away someday soon. But without you, it would never have left me."

Balancing with one hand against the glass, I cradle his cheek with my free hand as he begins to slow his movement into my body. "I missed you so much, Ian."

"Promise me you'll never leave again," he says in a hoarse voice as he buries himself inside me and I feel his release flood my insides.

The sensation of him filling me sends me tumbling over the edge. Clinging to him as his cock pulses inside me, I swear to never leave him again. "I promise. Never."

His hips slow their thrusting, and in a whisper I barely hear, he says, "I love you, Kristina. Please don't leave me."

Ian slides out of my body and wraps his arms around me as he gently places kisses on my cheek. Leaning back, I rest my head on his chest and listen to his heartbeat as it gradually returns to normal after our lovemaking.

"I love you, Ian," I say quietly as he strokes my hair. "And I'm sorry. I should have never run away like I did."

"I told you we'd see one another again. I never doubted it."

As he continues to gently caress me, I think back to that message he sent the night I left him. Had he truly never doubted that we'd see each other again? For all my belief that I'd loved him before, it wasn't until I missed him that I realized how deeply I needed him. Had he felt that before

I left?

✦   ✦   ✦

WE LIE IN his bed silently holding one another as the last remnants of the pain and sadness of the past week slip away. I think about how much I missed him—his touch, his voice, his eyes when he looks at me like he can't go on without me. I don't want to lose him again. We're both messed up. I know that. But can't messed up people be happy too?

I want that so much—to be happy just like we are at this moment. With my head rested on his chest, I trace my fingertip down over his lean stomach to the thin, dark line of hair that leads to his cock. Touching the soft down, I feel his skin tremble beneath my fingers and look up at him to see a smile on his face.

"Were you sleeping?"

"Not exactly, but all it takes is one touch of your hand on me and I'm wide awake."

"Is it early?" I ask, unsure if I've even slept this night.

Ian leans over toward the night table to see his alarm clock and groans. "Not even six yet. Go back to sleep."

"You don't want me to…?" I leave my question incomplete, but he pulls me up to kiss me on the lips.

"Later. Now I just want to feel you in my arms."

His disinterest in sex strangely makes me happy. I'd worried more than once that everything we are revolves around our physical connection, but with his refusal of me going down on him I feel like our emotional connection is at least as meaningful to him as it is to me.

"Unless you really want to twist my arm."

I hear the teasing in his voice and smile. "Just so I'm clear on this, we aren't just sex, are we?"

My attempt at being lighthearted falls flat. His expression hardens, and he asks, "Do you think all I care about is fucking you?"

"No, no," I protest, but it's too late. I've ruined everything. "I'm sorry. I didn't mean to make it sound like that."

Taking my face in his hands, he cradles my cheeks and kisses me on the tip of my nose. "I don't want you to ever think that. Tell me you know that."

I nod. "I do. I didn't mean to ruin our nice time together. I'm sorry."

"Don't be sorry, Kristina. You didn't ruin anything. I guess it's natural to wonder if all we are is sex since it's so incredible between us."

"It's just never been like this for me before

with anyone."

"I'll take that as a compliment."

Ian's lack of mention about my sexual abilities makes me want to ask if he's had a relationship like this before, but I'm afraid to know the answer. What if sex is always like this for him and I'm nothing special?

I nuzzle his neck and silently hope that our time together is important to him, inhaling the earthy, masculine scent of his skin. He smooths his hand over my hair and down my back, and as if he can read my mind, whispers in a deep voice, "No one has ever made me crave them like you do. I'm lost when you're not around, but I'm only slightly better when you're next to me and I want so fucking bad to be inside you."

The way he professes his need for me makes me want to please him. I want him to love me like no man ever has before. Like every man always said they did.

Ian stirs under me, gently pushing me off him as he slips out of bed. Still naked, he flashes me a smile. "I'll be right back. I want you to hear something."

My gaze is fixed on his very grabbable ass as he walks across the bedroom floor to head out to the living room. Lean and strong, his body looks like it's built to please a woman. A gentle ache settles in between my legs as I remember how his ass felt as I squeezed it just before my orgasm tore through me the last time we made love.

As I daydream about Ian's body, he returns with his laptop and slides back into bed next to me. "I want to read you what I wrote yesterday."

"Okay. What part is this?"

As he types something, he looks down at me next to him and smiles. "The end."

Surprised, I sit up and snuggle his arm. "You finished it?"

"Yeah. I couldn't write the whole time you were gone, but as soon as you began to text me, it was like I couldn't stop the words from coming." He kisses the top of my head and adds, "I couldn't do it without my muse."

Just hearing those words makes my heart fill with joy. I'm still his muse and he needs me. Nothing could make me happier at this moment. I look up at him and gaze into those nearly jet black eyes so intent on the words he's written as they wait for him on the screen.

"I can't wait for you to hear this. I created a male character halfway through, so I had to double back to the beginning, but as I reached what I thought was the end, something felt like it was missing, so I had his character end the book instead of Kate's."

"What's his name?"

"Sean."

"This sounds vaguely familiar to someone I know. Don't you think?"

I know what he's done. His story about me has morphed into the story of us. And I love him for it.

The sheepish look on his face charms me. Pressing my cheek to his shoulder, I lean over and curl my arm around his as he begins to read me the words he's given to Kate's hero, Sean.

"I put the two of them in a situation where they had to do without one another, and until you texted me today, I couldn't find the words I needed to bring them back together. They just sat there, lonely and alone, and then I suddenly knew what to say. So here's their reunion I wrote before I asked you to come back to me."

She opens the door, and for the first time in what feels like months I see her. Her deep blue eyes that make me feel like I could get lost in them and be happy for the rest of my life. Her gentle smile that belies the sensual woman I know her to be. Her body, the taut and toned muscles my touch remembers that make my cock hard even before I know if she'll take me back.

Her delicate mouth—those lips that have taken me to places of ecstasy like no other woman has ever done—she opens her mouth to speak, but for a moment says nothing. Has she changed her mind?

"Sean."

She speaks my name like a gentle plea, and I step forward to take her into my arms, needing to feel her next to me. Resting her head on my chest, she whispers, "I missed you so much."

I caress her back as she quietly sobs against me. "I'm sorry, Kate. I'm sorry I fucked up."

"Tell me you can accept who I am," she begs, looking up at me with a look in those gorgeous blue eyes that practically breaks my heart in two. "Tell me what I am is enough."

Cradling her face in my hands, I struggle to choke back the emotion she creates in me. I'm supposed to be the man, the one she turns to when she needs someone strong to hold her up, but I left her when she needed me most. What kind of fucking man does that?

"Baby, I love every part of you. The good part that makes me believe in the sweetness life can offer when you find the person you're meant to be with. The bad part that other men can't handle but I can't do without. I love all of you."

Kate closes her eyes and hangs her head. "You deserve someone who's more good than bad. That's not me."

I can't let her torment herself like this. She deserves to know how much I need her. Tilting her head so she looks up at me, I kiss her softly, like a whisper, and begin saying what I should have said the moment I knew how much I loved her.

"My beautiful, broken girl, you can't see what you are to me? I need you more than the air I breathe or the food I eat to survive. The whole time you weren't by my side, I felt like a part of me was missing, like someone had taken away a part of my being and left a gaping hole nothing could fill. You're everything to me."

"Why if I ruin that?" she asks, the fear filling her eyes.

"I won't let you ruin what we have, baby. I'll be strong enough for both of us. I promise. I need you too much to lose you."

Ian stops reading and turns to look at me. "It's a first draft, but I like how it's turning out."

Sitting up, I kiss him deeply, trying to convey how much I love what he's written. When I pull away, he smiles at me and I know he understands.

"So they live happily ever after?" I ask, hoping Kate and Sean get that at the end of their story.

He shakes his head. "Not quite yet. I thought I only had one story in me, but as I neared the end, I realized I didn't want to finish their story, so there will be a Silk Two."

"Another book? Will I be your muse for that one too?"

Placing the laptop on the nightstand next to him, Ian kisses me. "I can't do this without you, Kristina."

Hearing him say that makes what I felt just a few hours ago meaningless. People in love do stupid things. I left Ian because I was afraid, and he slept with someone to try to forget me. Both of us didn't want to admit the truth of who we are together.

I need him as much as he needs me. That's what love is with us.

CHAPTER FIVE

Ian

WHEN KRISTINA LEAVES just before nine a.m., I feel like I'm walking on air. I've written a complete book without heroin. The one soul on this earth I love is back in my life, and the words that had been trapped inside me now flow freely again.

I can't help thinking life is good.

And then at just after noon, it gets even better. Someone knocking at my door rouses me from my focus on plotting out the second Silk book, and when I answer it I see Sheila standing there in all her glory. Dressed in a yellow sweater and a gunmetal grey skirt that seems to accentuate all her rough edges, she's not exactly a sight for sore eyes, but I know if she's come all the way to my apartment she has good news about something. Plus, she's holding a bottle in her hands, which tells me it's likely very good news.

"Ian," she says with a huge smile as she

marches past me into my home. "I bring good news. Where should I sit?"

Closing the door, I follow her into the living room and offer her a chair I never use. "Please, sit. What good news?"

Sheila sits and awkwardly folds her long legs to the left, but the effect is almost grotesque and I can't take my eyes off how large and bulbous her kneecaps are. For a moment, I'm unable to concentrate as I wonder if I've ever seen knees like hers. She's already talking by the time I regain my focus, so I'm forced to admit I need her to repeat what she's just said.

"Sorry, Sheila. You lost me there for a second. Can you start from the top?"

Her face twists into a look of suspicion as she narrows her eyes. "Have you been...?" Her question trails off, and I know she's afraid to finish the last part because of what my answer might be.

I shake my head. "No, I haven't been doing anything like that. I promise. I just lost my focus for a second. Nothing big. Just early in the day for me."

She's silent for a long moment, almost like she's mentally weighing the veracity of my statement against how I look, but then she smiles. "Okay. As I was saying, the publisher loves the idea of Marc Antony. Seems he's all the rage because of some biopic that's due to come out early next year. I had no idea about it when I told you to basically shelve the idea, of course. I hope you won't hold that against me."

I wave my hand in the air. "No bad feelings. Everyone's entitled to their opinions. I know you love my work and how much you've done to get it out there."

"I really have, and I think the publisher is thrilled to be having this to run with. I hope you can begin immediately. They want this for next fall's releases. That means you literally have weeks, Ian. Weeks. Can you do it?"

Real fear settles into my brain at her words. Weeks. A Marc Antony book will take weeks or months just to research, even if I do decide to go with a similar format to my past two historical fiction novels.

"How long do I really have?" I ask knowing I likely have months instead of weeks.

"Maybe three months," she says in the most somber tone she's ever used with me about writing. I know what's coming next. "Is that going to put too much pressure on you, Ian?"

Her question is like a life size reality check dropped into the center of the room. I practically have to lean to the side to see her it's taking up so much space between us. The fact is I've never been very good under pressure after the book's been written. Adding pressure to the normal stress of writing a book sounds like a recipe for disaster, I'm sure.

But I'm different now. I have Kristina, and I don't think about snorting that shit up my nose every other minute of the day. For the first time since I wrote my first book, I know I can write without the junk coursing through my veins.

I can't tell Sheila any of this, though. Kristina must remain my secret. So I do my best to convince my agent that I won't become a doped up mess over this book. "I'll be fine. Months is very different than weeks. I'm more concerned with the research required for a Marc Antony book. Guess this means I'll be heading back to Rome."

A sheepish look crosses her face. "They won't give you the advance until you submit the manuscript, though, Ian. I'm sorry. I tried. I really did. But I couldn't fight them with much when they threw your past in my face. I really am sorry."

The truth of who I am stings, but she's not to blame. Either is my publisher. My past isn't going to disappear simply because I say it should. "I understand, Sheila."

"I was able to get you a very healthy advance of $75,000, though, when the book is submitted. I hope that helps a little."

"It does," I say, admitting while it's the smallest advance I've ever received, especially after having two bestselling books, it's not bad considering what's happened in the past.

"And they want a book tour this time. Well, actually, I convinced them that a book tour would be a great thing. They were hesitant to agree after what happened on the Caligula's Dream tour, but I told them those days are behind you."

I see the fear in her eyes as she talks about my first and last book tour. I'd fucked that up royally, for sure. Ten cities in two weeks and I'd barely made it through three signings before I fell apart and the rest of the dates had to be cancelled. Cringing as I remember her showing up in my hotel room with two of Albert's assistants to whisk me out of the building before anyone else found out how much a mess I was, I hang my head in shame. She really does take care of me, and until recently, I've been little more than a hassle.

"Thank you, Sheila. I really mean that. I know I've been a lot of trouble, and the fact that my books do well doesn't make up for what you've had to deal with in the past."

A smile brightens her face making her almost

appealing. "As long as you're taking care of yourself and not doing that terrible stuff anymore, I'm happy. You're one of my favorite authors, Ian."

I think she's telling the truth, as hard as that is to believe. As she hands me the bottle of champagne to open, she adds, "And at least I don't have to worry about you sounding off on Twitter or Facebook, for God's sake. Just that alone makes you a treasure in my book."

Walking into the kitchen, I ask, "Is your newbie author doing any better?"

"No," she yells from the living room, "and I'm seriously thinking she's enjoying the notoriety she's receiving from angering people. I think she actually believes that nonsense of there being no bad publicity."

I pop the cork and return to my seat with the open bottle and two champagne glasses. Placing them on the table, I pour each of us a drink to toast her great work for me. "Not in this business. Your reputation is everything in the book business. I learned that the hard way."

Sheila takes her glass and lifts it in the air. "But you learned. I'm worried this one isn't interested in learning from her mistakes."

Raising my glass, I make an apropos toast. "To learning from one's mistakes before it's too late."

"Hear, hear!" she says with a smile before she takes a sip of champagne. "So now for the question I have to ask, Ian. Have you written anything for the Marc Antony project?"

I know I'm fortunate enough to have some good in my history with my publisher, which means I don't need much more than Sheila's first-rate agenting skills to persuade them on a project. The problem that creates is that I don't need to write anything, not even a synopsis, before they agree to run with an idea. Now that they've said yes, the writing has to begin immediately.

Deciding to answer with the truth, I shake my head. "Not yet. But I've got a lot of ideas, so there's no need to worry. You can count on me. As we've been talking, I've already been planning a trip to Rome and what I'm thinking the story will be about."

Sheila lets out a heavy sigh, as if my answer has taken the weight of the world off her shoulders. "That's good. That's what I want to hear. Well, actually, I would have loved it if you said you'd already begun work on this, but I'll take planning over nothing."

"What is it they say? Baby steps? I promise I won't let you down."

I finish my glass of champagne quickly,

knowing that she's eagle-eyeing every move I make, and place my empty glass on the table even though I want another drink. I don't need to have her worrying about my alcohol consumption too.

"I believe you. I do. I just worry. You know how I am. All my authors are like my children, so I worry about all of you. I like to think that's what makes me such a good agent."

"You're a great agent. Don't ever doubt that because we're assholes who don't know how to behave."

My sudden expression of caring makes her uneasy, and she shifts in her seat. "You're not an asshole, Ian. You're one of my favorites. It's just that with your issues—" She doesn't finish her sentence, as always uncomfortable saying the word heroin.

"I'm better now. I promise. I wrote all of Nero's Nightmare without the heroin, so I'm good now, Sheila."

Leaning forward, she places her glass on the table. "Good. I'm happy to hear that, Ian. I really am." She rises from the chair and flings her purse over her shoulder. "I'll leave you so you can begin working on Marc Antony's story. You're going to go to Rome again, but call me after you get back."

I walk her to the door. "I will. As soon as I get back."

In her typical fashion, she pulls me to her in a bear hug and whispers in my ear, "I know this one will be great too. Don't forget that if the going gets tough I'm just a phone call away."

As she releases me, I smile at her kindness. "I won't. And thanks again for coming by. I'll talk to you soon."

Sheila walks away with a pleased look on her face that tells me she believed what I'd said. Not that I'd lied, but I can't deny how much I'd had to pretend for her. It was all for the best anyway. If I told her about Kristina and Silk, it would just cause her more grief, and I don't want to be that for her anymore.

Eager to put that thought out of my mind, I busy myself with preparations for the trip to Rome. I need to make air and hotel reservations, along with contacting Dr. Farelli again. Hopefully, his secretary still likes me well enough to let me past her or I'd have to sic Albert on her again.

I can't wait to tell Kristina about the trip. During the day, I'll conduct my research while she shops or visits tourist attractions, and afterward we'll have dinner in the finest restaurants and take long walks to the Trevi Fountain and the Forum where I'll tell her the history of the city and all about my previous trips there.

Everything finally had turned the corner. My work. My private life. Everything.

CHAPTER SIX

Kristina

M Y PUBLICIST CALLS me just as I'm on my way home to tell me she has to see me. Joanne sounds hyper on most days, but today her voice reminds me of an old style record put on the wrong speed or some overexcited cartoon chipmunk. I'm barely able to understand her, but I agree to see her, knowing if I don't that she'll simply call Jennie, my agent, and God knows I don't need her worry piling on top of my happiness.

During my cab ride to Joanne's office, I think about my reunion with Ian. Finally, after all my silliness, we're back together. But I can't help silently admit to myself that even thinking about him comes with a shadow of hurt from knowing he slept with that other woman.

I imagine what she looks like since all I know about her is how she sounds while Ian was inside her. I hate the fact that all I know about her is something so intimate yet I don't even know her name or what color hair she has. In my mind's eye, I see her as a blond. Yes, she must be a blond so she can be different from me. No, a fake, platinum blond so she's the opposite of what I look like. And she has beady little eyes and mascara that clumps on her skimpy eyelashes.

Is her hair long like mine? Did he bury his hands in her hair as they made love and tug, sending a mix of pain and pleasure down her spine like he does when he pulls my hair? Did she enjoy it like I do, or did she tell him to stop hurting her?

Quickly, my mind spirals out of control with images of them together. His eyes staring into hers as he enters her, their darkness seeming to fill his entire eyes as passion takes him over. His lips kissing her neck and breasts as he murmurs the sexiest, dirtiest thoughts he has. His hands sliding down her side and grabbing her hips as he pumps his cock into her.

Shaking my head, I struggle to push the images out of my mind. No! I can't think like this. I can't let my insecurities overrun me until all that's left of what I have with him is petty jealousy. I left him. Left him with no explanation. I did this to us. If I wanted Ian to be mine, I had to accept my responsibility for him ending up with another woman. If I wanted us to work out, I had to face my fears and self-doubts.

I had to stop running away.

The cab stops in front of Joanne's building, and as I hop out onto the sidewalk, I take a deep breath to clear my head. I can be the woman Ian thinks I am, the sensual woman he professed his love to and wrote that beautiful story for. All I need to do is believe in myself. He loves me, and I love him.

Now to deal with my publicist.

Joanne Jenkins has been my publicist since I began in this business, and in all the time I've known her, her office hasn't changed. It's still that tiny white box with walls cluttered from too many framed clippings in newspapers and magazines. The rest of the world may be online, but not her. For Joanne, life still revolves around getting mentioned in gossip columns people can hold in their hands and stuff into their briefcases and purses.

Her assistant sits outside her office at an old desk that reminds me of the kind the woman at the DMV in my hometown in Indiana sat at the day I went in to take my driving test. Metal and tan, it makes a hollow noise every time her knees bang into it. Charlene is a lovely person, but I can't imagine how someone so jittery can work with another so hyper person such as Joanne. It's almost as if they create too much energy for the tiny space they occupy.

A pretty woman with a round face, Charlene has the kind of blond hair I imagined a few minutes ago for the woman Ian had sex with, and I find it hard not to frown as I approach her today. She sees me and with her usual perkiness says, "Kristina, it's so wonderful to see you! Joanne will be just a few minutes, so please take a seat. How is everything going?"

I look around at the chairs near her desk and choose the one farthest away. "Fine. Everything's fine."

"That's great! Let me buzz Joanne and see what's holding her up."

I want to say it hasn't even been thirty seconds since she told me she'd be a few minutes, but I don't, instead choosing to just smile. Joanne answers her in a sharp tone unmistakable over the loudspeaker and before Charlene can begin to talk me up again, my publicist appears in her doorway waving her hand to beckon me in.

She ushers me into her tiny office and begins talking before I can even sit down in front of her desk. Excited about some gossip concerning another actress, she rambles on and I catch bits and pieces as I try to get my bearings. I've spent so much time with Ian recently that I've gotten used to the calmness he projects. Between Charlene and Joanne, I feel like I'm being assaulted on all sides. I don't know how much my psyche can take of them today.

"So I wanted to talk to you about Vancouver. Have you heard anything yet? What do you think?" she asks in Gatling gun fashion.

Shaking my head, I say, "No, not yet. I hope to hear something this week, though."

Joanne flips her hand through her brunette bob and pops a stick of gum into her mouth. "Okay, well when you hear anything, we need to promote the hell out of this. You've been entirely too quiet lately, and I don't like that. I want the press to be dying to get at you."

"I've just been taking some down time, Joanne. The public understands that."

"The public understands nothing but what we feed them, Kristina. I thought you knew that. If we tell them you've been sick, we'll get sympathy. If we tell them you just needed time off, we'll get resentment at the idea that an actress needs time off. They don't understand that becoming an entirely different person for their amusement is hard work."

"I think you might just see the glass half empty," I say, half-joking and half-serious.

"Call me Machiavellian, but I understand the public, honey. I've been doing this since you were an innocent baby out there in the Midwest. Do you remember Eliza Gibson?"

Quickly, I try to remember hearing that name somewhere, but I can think of nothing. "No. Who's she?"

"She was an actress who decided that her career shouldn't dictate her entire existence. Foolish girl! I warned her. I told her the public has a very short attention span and even shorter memory. I told her they'd forget her if she didn't tend to her career like a careful gardener tends to his garden. She wouldn't listen. She needed some time off to get her head together or some bullshit like that. And before she knew it, she was yesterday's news and there was nothing I could do to fix that."

I can't help but roll my eyes. Some down time between projects and Joanne already thinks I'm on my way to becoming a has-been. "It's not the same, and you know it."

Her arms flail out to the sides of her head. "What I know is my job, and my job is to keep you front and center so Middle America doesn't forget you."

"What would you have me do? It's only been a few months. I can't help it that I'm not a drug addict or alcoholic in and out of rehab every other month."

Joanne leans forward and sighs. "I wish we could have gotten more mileage out of that John Stinson business."

Her mention of my public humiliation and being left brokenhearted as if it was something good makes me cringe. Looking down toward my lap, I say in a low voice, "Sorry my misery didn't last long enough for you."

"Well, whatever it was for you privately, it was a boon professionally. The public loves a tragic story, and that son of a bitch served us up one on a silver platter. You should thank him for that, dear."

"I'll make sure to do that the next time I see him with the woman he dumped me for," I mumble.

"Cheer up! Men are a dime a dozen in this world. Just look at me. I've been married three times. Divorced three times too, but the possibility of number four is always right around the corner. As long as someone like you picks men who can help her when it ends, that's all that matters."

My publicist continues to talk about the sad ending of my relationship with John, but I tune her out, preferring to think about how happy I am with Ian. As different from that bastard as night from day, he's thoughtful and sensual. John was just a good looking stud who never cared about anything but getting laid and moving up the ladder of success.

I wish I could tell her about Ian to prove to her I'm not some pathetic mess who needs to be torn apart to stay interesting to the movie-going public. My relationship with Ian makes me happy and proud, but I know the dangers of letting the world know about us. He can't afford that, even if it would help me.

"So I want you to let me know the minute you hear anything about the part. I want to get the news out there and blanket the media with it. You're on the verge of becoming a huge movie star, Kristina. We don't want to lose a minute of the spotlight."

"I will. Don't worry."

I get up to leave, exhausted and on the verge of feeling like shit after our meeting, but she stops me and almost as an afterthought says, "And if you get together with anyone, make sure he's famous, would you? It would make a world of difference. Too many stars are hooking up with nobodies these days, and I can't tell you how hard it is to spin gold out of something like that."

"Thanks, Joanne. I'll keep that in mind as I

look for love," I say, my words dripping with sarcasm she seems to miss entirely.

"Good, good, good. Tell Jennie I said hi and to take my calls every so often."

"I will."

Happy to be away from the emotional chaos of Joanne and her rapid fire talking, I head over to my agent's office a few blocks away. A few years younger but in an entirely different league professionally than my publicist, Jennie's never liked her, and I think I'm beginning to see why. I can totally understand why she'd not want to take her calls.

For Jennie, her place in my professional life is less one of orders and directions and more one of support. That she's entirely worried I'm going to leave her at any moment for another agent doesn't lessen how much I like her. And compared to my friends' agents, she's a gem.

Her office is only slightly bigger than my publicist's, but the dimensions have been rendered meaningless because of the way she's arranged it. The beige walls are practically bare, with just a sparse collection of framed nature photos hanging on them. At first glance, her wooden desk and workstation seem like they're too big for such a small space, but they're the only furniture someone sees as they sit there with her because she's cleverly turned a closet at the back of the room into a walk-in bookcase. So while she works in very much the same size office as Joanne, the effect couldn't be more different.

Jennie extends her well-manicured hand out to shake mine as I'm shown in to her office. "Kristina, how are you? You look wonderful and completely rested. Whatever you're doing, it's working."

"Thank you. I feel good. I'm ready to go back to work, so I hope you have good news for me."

Her plum colored lips hitch up at the corners into a gentle smile that goes all the way to her dark green eyes, letting me know she's genuinely happy to tell me what she has to say. "I do. Your audition blew them away. I knew it would, but they made their decision this morning. They want you, Kristina. The part of Cherise is yours, if you want it."

This is what I've been waiting to hear for weeks. I'd auditioned for the part of Cherise Johnson, a down-on-her-luck prostitute trying to change her life in spite of the man she loves doing everything in his power to keep her under his control and weak, but I'd considered myself a longshot for the part, at best. Bigger names than me had expressed interest in the role, and I worried I looked too Midwest, white bread for it.

I'd shown up to the audition in costume, fully ready to show them I was Cherise Johnson, and even though I'd thought it had gone well, I still didn't feel sure I'd convinced them I could do it.

I believed I could, though, and now that I'd get the chance, I'd show everyone I could do it.

"That's wonderful, Jennie! I'm so happy," I said, barely able to contain my giddiness at the news.

"Shooting begins in a few weeks in Vancouver, so get yourself packed and ready to go. They're sending everything over by courier later today, so once it all gets here, you can sign on the dotted line and the deal with be made. You're going to be incredible, Kristina. I just know it."

"I think so too," I say, not caring for once that I sound like I'm bragging.

"This could be it—the big break you've been looking for. This role has everything. You're really going to get the chance to stretch your limits with this one. You beat out some big names."

The way she says that makes me think she's most impressed by that fact. Hilary Swank and Natalie Portman had been the frontrunners the last time I heard, and knowing I got the role instead of them thrills me more than I could say. It seems to thrill Jennie too.

"I know. I can't believe it now that it's sunken in."

"Finally, a role to show them your chops. I've been waiting for a role like this for you since you came to me, you know that?"

"Thank you, Jennie. You always believed in me. That means so much to me."

"You promise when they announce your name for the Oscar you won't drop me for a flashier agent out there in LA?" she asks, her expression suddenly far more serious than it was a minute ago.

I know this is one of her biggest fears. Since I signed with her, she's worried almost constantly about me leaving her for another agent. Not that I would. I like her in my professional life. Compared to virtually everyone else who surrounds me, she feels like the calm in the middle of a storm. That's too important to me to lose.

"I'm not going anywhere, Jen. You've stuck with me through minor roles and critics saying I wasn't living up to the hype and my looks. If this role means doors begin to open for me, I'm going to be going through them with you. I don't want another agent. They're all too much like Joanne."

Jennie makes a noise that sounds like pure disgust at the mention of my publicist. "I know she's been with you nearly as long as I have, but her vision for you troubles me. She loved the media circus that came from your breakup with John. I can't tell you how many times she called me to discuss how we could use this to further your career."

I shrug and try to act nonchalant about the one topic I'd rather not discuss. "Joanne sees things from a different perspective, I guess."

My agent screws her face into an expression of disgust. "She's like an ambulance chaser." Quickly, she holds up her hands and shakes her head. "I'm sorry. That's not appropriate for me to say. I just didn't like the glee she seemed to feel at your heartbreak."

"It's over now, so it's all in the past. I'm onto bigger and better things," I say with a smile, genuinely feeling good.

Jennie levels her gaze on me. "Are we still talking about your career or something else here?"

I want to share how happy I am with Ian, but my promise to him to keep our relationship private echoes in my ears. So I tell a lie, more a sin of omission really. "My career, of course, but I'm feeling really good about my personal life too. I'm over that John mess and ready for a new love."

"That's what I love to hear! Just keep that positive attitude and I know things will work out.

Now get yourself home and start packing. I'll give you a call when I get the papers."

"Okay." Extending my hand, I shake hers and say, "Thanks so much again, Jennie. I couldn't have gotten this without your help."

She takes me into her arms for a hug. "Nonsense. I'm just the messenger. You're the one they're dying to work with, so go show them what you got, kid."

I leave her office feeling like I'm walking on air. This film is my big chance. After years of working hard at my craft and taking roles other actresses saw as beneath them, I finally had the opportunity to break out and show the world what I could do with my talent.

But what about Ian and me? The idea of leaving him for months to go shoot a movie in Vancouver makes me break out in a cold sweat. One week we were apart and he slept with another woman. But that was because I left him, I remind myself.

But I'll be leaving him now too. He's become so much a part of my life that imagining it without him scares the hell out of me. What if he doesn't want to wait for me?

I hurry to his apartment to see him, debating all the way there whether I should tell him my good news or not. I know he'll be happy for me because he loves me, but it's so early in the relationship to be apart for so long. He answers his door and I throw my arms around him, already missing the feel of his body next to mine.

"Kristina, what's wrong? Did something happen?" he asks, not knowing how much my good news is torturing me at that moment.

"I missed you. That's all."

Closing the door, he takes me by the hand to the couch and practically beaming says, "I have wonderful news. My publisher agreed to the Marc Antony book, so I need to travel to Rome to research before I begin writing. What do you say to a month in the Eternal City?"

His eyes are wide with excitement as he tells me his good news, and I can't bring myself to say no, even though I know there's no way I can take this trip with him and begin work on the film at the same time. As he waits for my answer, I see how much this means to him, so I nod and smile as I tell him I can't wait for our trip together.

"As soon as I knew I'd be going there again, I looked into making reservations for us. Oh, Kristina, you're going to love it there. We'll see the sights and it will be the best trip I've ever had to Rome."

He describes all the plans he's making, and all I can think is how he included me in them without any prodding from me. No man has ever put me first like this. How am I going to ever tell him I can't go because of my work?

"And I have another surprise for you. Silk is ready. I'm going to self-publish it tonight or tomorrow. Our story isn't going to be just ours anymore."

"What does that mean? Aren't you going to use a pseudonym?"

"Yes, but as a writer, I know once a story is published, it no longer really stays mine. I have no idea if anyone will want to read it or even be able to find it, but it's ready."

I kiss him and swipe a dark stray lock of hair from his forehead. "I know people are going to love it. How couldn't they? You wrote it."

"Maybe I'm not a very good writer if it's not historical fiction," he says in a voice that makes me think he truly isn't sure about readers loving our story.

I trace the outline of his lower lip and lean in to gently suck it into my mouth. Giving it a tiny nip, I see the desire in his eyes and let go. "You're a great writer all the time, Ian, and the story you've told in Silk is sensual and erotic. I just know people will love it."

Sliding his hands down to cup my ass, he pulls me to him and I feel his already hard cock.

"I'd planned on telling you all about the plans I'm making for our trip, but that can wait. Right now, I'd rather be balls deep inside you than talk about anything else."

"More research for your writing?"

Ian shakes his head as he sensually drags his lips down my neck. "Not exactly."

I don't stop him, and for a few moments I'm able to push the reality of what I have to tell him out of my mind. His love for me comes through in every touch of his hand and every kiss. Gently, he pulls my skirt down my body and kneeling in front of me, Ian looks up with his dark eyes and gives me one of his sexy smiles I love so much.

"I can't tell you how happy I am that I get to spend time in one of my favorite places in the world with the woman I love."

As he slides his hands up my thigh and presses his lips to my sex, my body begins to soar. I want to be able to lose myself in him like always, but I can't forget that at some point I'm going to have to tell him the truth and ruin all his plans.

CHAPTER SEVEN

Ian

WHEN I TOLD Kristina I wasn't even sure anyone would find Silk, I wasn't kidding. Forget about the needle in the haystack. Selling a book online seems akin to the task of finding one particular tiny piece of hay in a haystack. How anyone sells any real number of books baffles me, but Sheila had said that some authors were doing it, so I figure I'll jump in with both feet and upload Silk to all the major sales outlets that sell my historical fiction books and will take my self-published one.

It's almost too easy. I know nothing about formatting a book to be published, but with a little reading about it online, I'm ready to go. I agree to read a friend's book in exchange for a simple very sexy cover and then it's time to upload.

For two days I watch our book just sit there as nobody finds it. I'm not really surprised given the nature of the major sites. Again, Silk is just one tiny piece of hay in their big haystacks. Then on the third day, there's one sale. One. As I check the sales totals each day, I have to wonder how anyone makes any kind of living this way.

It's definitely not something that grows organically, but for my first foray into erotica, I'm happy. A few more people buy it, and slowly reviews trickle in that show readers loving Kate and Sean as much as I loved writing them. It's no bestseller, but I'm pleased.

Then just about five days after it's published, I happen to be surfing through the channels as I wait for Kristina one night and see a reporter on one of the entertainment news shows say that actress Kristina Richards mentioned the book she's reading now is Silk. Stunned to hear that, I ask her about it when she arrives.

"They were asking me bunches of questions. Did you see the whole thing? What part did you see?" she asks in an excited voice as I pour her a glass of wine.

"Not much. Just the part about the book. Was there anything else they asked you that I should know about?"

Taking the glass from my hand, she shakes her head and asks in a shaky voice, "Like what? What else would they ask me?"

She's nervous. It's clear in the way she's acting, but I don't know why. "You didn't say anything about us, did you?"

Kristina sighs, visibly relieved by my question. "No, no. Is that what you were worried about? I told you I won't say anything."

"Did you say you knew the author of Silk?" I press further, still wondering why she was so nervous a minute ago.

"No. I just mentioned it in the hopes that maybe if they included that on their program that it could help it get seen. Has it?"

"Not in any appreciable way yet," I say with a smile, still incredulous about how anyone makes a living as an author this way.

Kristina gives me a tiny kiss and smiles up at me. "I'm not a huge name, so maybe nobody cares what I read in my spare time. The interviewer did ask me what it was about, so I told her. Did they include that in the show?"

"No, not that I saw. It might have helped. You know what they say. Sex sells."

My joke makes her giggle and she nuzzles my neck. "Mmmm...yes it does."

Taking her in my arms, I kiss the tender skin just below her ear and ask, "Have you been thinking about our trip? Are you excited about it?"

Her neck and shoulders tense up, and I lift my head to see her beautiful blue eyes clouded over. She forces a smile, but something's wrong. I can see it. Nodding, she answers, "I haven't thought much about it yet, but I'm very excited. I've never been to Rome."

I want to break the tension that's settled in between us, although I have no idea why it has, so I ask, "Not even for a film? I thought movie stars travelled around the world."

Scrunching up her face, she says, "Some might, but I haven't yet."

There's a pregnant pause as I watch her silently struggle to decide whether or not she wants to continue talking. She's hiding something from me, but what? Backing away from her, I lean against the counter and fold my arms across my chest.

"Is something wrong, Kristina?"

"No. Why would something be wrong?"

Every person in the world who has something they're hiding has asked that question in response to being asked if something is wrong. I don't know what it is, but if she won't tell me, my gut says it's bad. I walk past her into the living room, hoping that when she follows me she'll tell me what's wrong.

I watch her as she comes toward me on the

couch. If any poker player ever had a tell like she does, they'd lose their shirt every hand. My girl is a terrible liar.

"Why did you walk away like that?" she asks as she sits down next to me, cuddling up to my side.

"Just seemed like the thing to do so we don't get into a fight tonight."

I turn to see her blue eyes wide with surprise. "What would we fight about? I don't understand."

Studying her body language, I believe her, strangely enough. The worried tone in her voice says she doesn't understand what we'd fight about because I suspect she doesn't realize how clearly guilty she looks and whatever she's not telling me is much worse than the sin of omission she's committing.

"We promised to be truthful always, Kristina. Something in the way you're acting tells me you're not being truthful."

That sweetness I love in her slips away, leaving a frown on her beautiful mouth. "I think I better go."

"Wouldn't you rather just tell me what's wrong?"

She says nothing and stands to leave. "I have to go home, Ian."

Fuck if she hasn't called my bluff. I no more want her to leave than I want her to keep secrets from me, but if I have to choose between the two, I'll deal with the secrets if only she'll stay. I jump up from the couch and stop her.

"Don't go."

She hangs her head and whispers, "I have to. You don't trust me."

I don't want to let her go, but she tugs her hand from my hold, and for a long moment, I stand there watching her leave like the jackass I am as my mind plays tug of war over begging her to stay and letting her walk out.

With every step she takes, I feel like I'm losing part of myself. Why did I do this? Do I really need to know every thought she has every minute of the day? What am I? Some insecure teenage boy?

"Kristina, stay."

I walk toward the door to catch up with her, but something about her is different now. She doesn't want to stay.

"I'm sorry. I shouldn't have pushed like that. Stay and we can talk about Rome and how much fun we're going to have together there."

Kristina turns to face me with a look that chills my heart. Part anger, part sadness, her expression tells me I've made a mistake. "I'm going to go home now. I love you, but I need to go."

She leans forward and kisses me deeply, making me hate myself all the more for the bullshit I've caused tonight. I want to feel her beneath me as I make love to her. I want to show her I know I made a mistake and can make up for it.

I hold her hand, not ready for her to leave, and quietly say, "I'm sorry."

"I know. I am too. I'll call you tomorrow."

And with that, her fingers slip from my hold and she walks slowly to the elevator as I stand there knowing I fucked up. I could run after her and plead for her to come back, but my silent accusations have made her walls go up, and there's nothing I can do tonight to bring them down.

I OPEN MY eyes and how much I miss Kristina floods my brain before I can even put together a coherent thought about anything else. She should be next to me, making that adorable snoring noise she makes when she sleeps and blushing when she realizes I've been watching her and loving that cute pout her mouth does.

Scrubbing the sleep from my eyes, I stretch my arms and legs, missing the ache in my muscles from making love I always have after spending the night with her. God, I'm such a fuck!

The need to call her presses down on me, so I roll over and grab my phone from the nightstand. Three rings and the worry that I've fucked up worse than I thought begins to dawn on me. My call goes to voicemail and just hearing her gentle voice tell me she'll call me back as soon as she can makes me wince in pain.

I don't leave a voicemail and instead go straight for the text. Not that it's my best way of communicating by any means, but desperate times call for desperate measures. Tapping away with my thumbs, I do my best to tell her how much I miss her without unraveling emotions all over her phone.

I'm lying here in bed missing the feel of your body against mine.

She doesn't text back immediately, and my demons begin to take over. I'm sure she's with someone else. That guy she met at the bar she told me about. The guy who I saw kiss her on her doorstep that night. It doesn't matter who he is. He isn't me.

Five minutes later, I'm out of bed and dressed to go to her place. I screwed up and I know it, so I need to do something about it.

My phone vibrates against the top of the nightstand, and relief floods my mind. I look down to see her text back to me.

I miss you too.

Snatching my phone up, I quickly text back. *Come to me. We can spend all day in bed. I need you.*

I hit SEND and wait for her reply. Minute after minute ticks by, but she doesn't answer. I feel like she's punishing me, but if she is, I deserve it. I silently will my phone to vibrate like I have some control over any of it. Hell, I barely have control over myself.

After the tenth time of me telling my phone to give me her text, it vibrates and I look down to see what she's said.

I think it might be better for us to spend the day apart.

Each word feels like someone's stabbing me in the gut. Apart. I hadn't been wrong. She was hiding something from me.

Knowing me like she does, she has to expect me to do something. My legs move even before I make the decision to go to her. Grabbing my coat, I have to slow myself down so I don't run full speed directly to her apartment. As it is, I'm barely able to keep myself to a walk as my feet pound the sidewalk toward her building just blocks away.

Ten minutes later, I'm in front of the brownstone where her apartment is and look up to see her staring down at me from her living room window. She doesn't look frightened or angry that I'm there. And she doesn't look surprised.

If anything, she looks pleased to see me.

I tear up the stairs from the sidewalk and find the front door open for me. She unlocked it knowing I'd come. I take the stairs inside by twos and in less than a minute I'm at her door. I hear her. She's waiting for me to knock, to come to her.

Two sharp bangs on the door and she opens it. "Why are you here?"

"You know why. For the same reason you came to my apartment that other night."

She bites her lower lip and knits her brows like the thought causes her pain. "I don't want to think of that night."

"Let me in, Kristina. Let me show you how much I missed you."

Closing her eyes, she takes a deep breath in and lets it out, her shoulders sagging from her inability to stay angry at me. Without a word, she steps aside for me to come in.

I walk past and wrap my arms around her when she closes the door, needing to feel her against me. She doesn't move away to deny me this pleasure and leans her head back against my chest like she needs this too.

Quietly, in a small voice, she says, "Tell me how much you missed me."

Sliding my hand up the front of her neck, I feel the warmth of her skin against mine. I'm overcome with how much I missed this. Dipping my head, I press my lips to the shell of her ear and whisper, "I woke up this morning and my skin hurt because I needed you so much, but I didn't feel the ache I always feel after we make love."

She covers my hand with hers and whimpers softly as she arches her back. Her breasts graze my arm, and I feel her nipples hard from excitement. I love how responsive she is to my touch and my words.

"I feel like a part of me is missing when you aren't with me. Like someone's torn away something necessary and I can't go on without it, Kristina."

"Whatever this is we have between us makes me crazy, Ian."

Turning her to face me, I lift her chin so she has to look at me. "There's nothing wrong with being in crazy in love, Kristina."

"I don't want to be crazy. Crazy gets people hurt. I don't want to hurt you or have you hurt me."

I place a soft kiss on her lips and whisper, "Sometimes love hurts. That doesn't mean it isn't love."

She asks with a frown, "Why did you act like that toward me last night?"

I don't know why I acted like that. Because I thought she was lying. Because I worried she was holding something back. Pressing my forehead to hers, I answer her as truthfully as I can. "Because I'm fucked up and being with me means you see that. I just want to know you won't run away because of it."

"I would never hurt you intentionally, Ian." She leans her cheek against my hand and looks so sad. "I swear."

"I know. You're sweet and gentle and I'm a fucked up mess without you."

"Maybe we should take a couple weeks off."

Grabbing a fistful of her hair in my hand, I tug hard as my fears threaten to overrun me. Her eyes fill with tears, and I frantically say, "No. I don't want to take any time off from us, Kristina. Tell me you don't want to either."

"Please let go. You're hurting me!"

I loosen my hold on her hair and kiss her hard

on the lips. She fights against my kiss for a moment, but then her mouth softens and meets my passion with hers.

"Tell me you don't want us to end," I say with a lump in my throat. "Don't leave me, baby."

Kristina grabs at my shirt and tears it off me. Buttons fly everywhere and she sobs against my chest, "I hate the idea of losing you. I don't know what I'd do if I didn't have you."

"Then why did you say we should take some time off?" I ask as I begin to undress her.

Shaking her head, she fumbles with my pants to get them off while I tug her jeans down her legs. "I don't know. I don't know. I just thought maybe if we weren't together that we wouldn't get hurt."

We're caught up in this cycle of madness and need, and I know it's spinning out of control. I don't want to stop it, though. I can't. The idea of my world without Kristina makes me break out in a cold sweat. I need her. I love her. And even though I know she's hiding something, I don't care.

All I care about is being inside her.

She wraps her arms around my neck, clinging to me as I push her back against the hallway wall. Open and needy for me, her body envelopes me as I thrust my cock deep into her cunt. We fuck with abandon like Kate and Sean, and as she whimpers my name over and over, I begin to feel like I'm flying.

This is the high she gives me. The high I'm desperately addicted to. The high I can't do without.

Panting as I take her toward her orgasm, she pleads in my ear, "Ian, promise you won't ever let me go. Please promise."

The fear in her eyes warns of some problem we'll have to deal with eventually, but at that moment, I don't care. I don't care what she's done. All I care about is having her in my life. I grip her hips tightly as the first sweet squeeze of her cunt on my cock tells me she's just about there and answer in a groan, "I promise. I couldn't live without you."

She throws her head back as her release tears through her, and as she bucks wildly against me, I come with one last hard plunge into her, the two of us drenched in sweat and holding on to one another.

When her body ceases to tremble, she rests her head on my shoulder and says in barely a whisper, as if the words are too frightening to speak out loud, "I thought I could be without you. I was wrong. What are we going to do, Ian?"

I gently stroke her back. "There's nothing to

do. This is what we are."

I've never said more truthful words than those. There is nothing the two of us can do. Maybe her therapist was right and she becomes addicted to people. I thought that was bullshit psychobabble, but I'm as addicted to Kristina as I am to how she makes me feel. I don't know anymore. Nothing I've ever been addicted to ever felt like this.

✦   ✦   ✦

A LITTLE MORE than a week later, the story of our love exploded and hit the New York Times bestseller list. Silk by T. Anderson, some unknown erotica writer who self-published the story Kristina inspired that first night as I watched her movies and fell for her, hit #5.

I stand in my kitchen after letting her in and casually announce the news. "Silk hit the Times list."

Kristina's face is the purest example of confusion as my news sinks in. "Do you mean our book?"

My smile stretches wide at that. "Yes. Number five."

"Oh my God! Ian! That's wonderful! How, though? You used a pen name no one knows."

I take her in my arms and kiss her sweetly,

loving her naiveté. "You did this. First you inspired me and agreed to be my muse, and then you mentioned the book in that interview. That's what did it. My beautiful muse, you did this."

Kristina leans back and I see she has tears in her eyes. "I did this? Me?"

"All you."

Hugging me, she says, "Oh, Ian, I can't believe it. But it wasn't just me. Your story is why people bought it and made it a bestseller. It's you, not me."

I tip her head back and look down into those beautiful blue eyes I love. "It's us. We did this. And I think I'm going to write another one."

"Do you know what the story's about?"

"I don't know yet, but as long as I have my muse, I know it will be great."

She hugs me tightly to her again as I think about Rome and how the next chapter in our story will unfold. It will be there that the next book comes to be.

CHAPTER EIGHT

Kristina

I STAY IN bed late after three nights of celebrating Silk's success with Ian. What had begun as a torrid love affair has morphed into something so consuming, so part of me that even being away from him makes me uncomfortable. But I've done exactly what my therapist said to and let things happen naturally. It's just that natural for Ian and me isn't really natural.

In less than twenty-four hours, we're scheduled to fly to Rome, and I still haven't told him I can't go with him. I've tried. I really have. But every time I think it's the right moment to dash all his plans for us, he says something cute or funny about how much he's looking forward to our trip. How can I break his heart like that?

Closing my eyes, I curse my bad luck. For the first time ever, I have everything I want in life. It's just my luck that fate says I can't have it all at the same time. I can't turn down the role I've wanted so badly. That would be career suicide, and I'd be crazy to let that opportunity slip through my hands.

But the mere thought of losing Ian makes me feel hollow inside. If only I'd told him when I found out. Now when I have to ruin the Rome trip, he'll know I've been holding out on him and essentially lying for days and days. He gave me the chance to tell the truth that night, but like a fool I didn't take it.

Now I've made things ten times worse.

Desperate for some sound advice, I call Sienna. Unlike Priscilla, she always has clever ideas. She'll know what I should do.

"Kristina, I was just thinking about you," she says as she answers the phone.

"Really? Why?"

"A bunch of reasons. First is that guy I met that night when we went out just left my place. Oh my, that man knows how to fuck. Honey, you must get yourself someone like him."

I smile at the knowledge that I already have a man who knows just how to take care of me in that respect. Ian and I may be crazy together, but when it comes to sex, he's exactly what every man should be.

"I'm happy you're having a good time, Sienna."

"A good time doesn't even begin to describe it. All we do is fuck. I love it! He hasn't said anything about dating or a relationship and I couldn't be happier. Tell me things got better for you since that night. What happened with that banker you were talking to that night? Is he pinching your pennies these days?"

I can't help but giggle at the cute way she says things. Cute and blunt. "No, nothing happened. He just gave me a ride home. He wasn't really my type, you know?"

"Yeah, he did have a sort of boring thing going on. You're too sweet and fun for that kind of life. I'm not getting a three-piece suit and tie vibe for the kind of man you need. You need a little freakier, I think."

"I'll be sure to work on that, Sienna."

"So why are you calling me at eight a.m.? Did you just send some hot guy home?"

"No, nothing like that. I just needed some advice."

I hear the rustling of her sheets and comforter as she sits up to listen to what I have to say. "Advice? Is something wrong?"

"Yes and no. I need to figure out how to break bad news to someone."

"Do it like you tear off a Band-Aid—fast. Just say what you have to say and then deal with their reaction. How bad is the news we're talking about here?"

"Bad. It's going to disappoint this person a lot. I feel terrible about it too."

"Life is full of disappointment, Kristina. Adults deal. It isn't Cilla, is it?"

"No." That would be easy. Cilla can be difficult at times, but nothing ever seems to bother her for long. She's got a thoughtless streak in her that comes in handy at times like this.

"Because if it is her, I say do it slow and torture her. She left me hanging last weekend when I went out to LA to see her, so I'm still pissed at her."

"Sorry. I can't help you there. This isn't about her. It's about someone I really care for and don't want to hurt."

"That mystery man you were trying to get over that night we went out?" she asks, her voice full of curiosity.

I know I shouldn't mention anything even vaguely about Ian, but I say, "Yes, but I can't tell you any more than that about him."

"Nothing? You're not good at keeping secrets, Kristina. I'll get it out of you."

"Please don't try. It's bad enough I might be hurting him by giving him this bad news. I don't want to betray him too."

"Why would telling me about some guy betray him?" she asks now very curious.

"Because he asked me to keep our relationship a secret," I confess, knowing she'll think the worst, which she does.

"He's married. That's it. Married. He's a married son of a bitch who's cheating on his wife with you," she pronounces.

"He's not married," I say with a chuckle. If Ian is married, his wife sure doesn't seem to be much a part of his life.

"Are you sure? He doesn't want anyone to know about you two. Sounds like a married man to me."

"No, he's not married and I can't tell you any more about him. I just need to know how to break bad news without hurting him."

"Are you breaking it off with him?"

"No. I just need to cancel a trip we planned on taking because of work."

"Oh, that's not a big deal. You can take a trip anytime. Just tell him you need to reschedule."

If only it was that easy. I could have done that if I told him when I found out about Vancouver. Now it was too late.

"It's not that easy. I've lied for a while about it, saying I'd go. He has no idea."

"Why'd you do that?"

The explanation of why I'd made such a dumb choice would take too long, so I just mumble, "I don't know. I didn't want to disappoint him."

"So now you get to disappoint and hurt him. Well, I still say do it fast. Get it over with so you can move on to bigger and better things."

Sienna's words make my heart pound in my chest. I don't want to move on to anything. I just want to find a way to tell Ian that even though I love him I can't go to Rome like he wants. It sounds so simple when I say it in my head, but I know when I'm standing in front of him and I see the disappointment in those dark eyes of his that I'll feel terrible.

"Okay. Thanks Sienna. I guess I'll try it that way."

She squeals loudly into the phone, so I pull it away from my ear as she begins to talk about some show she's watching. Not exactly the way I wanted to begin my morning.

"Oh my God! Kristina! You're on Good Morning America!" I hear her scream.

Quickly, I pull the phone back to my ear as I search for the remote buried in the blankets. "What do you mean?"

"They're talking about your new film you begin shooting in Vancouver right now in their

Hollywood news segment. Did you put it on?"

My television turns on and there as big as life is my face in a box to the right of the pretty blond woman who reports on all things pop news and Hollywood gossip, including it seems me this morning. She's got all the details about the film and how I'll be there in just a few days.

"Is this what you were talking about, Kristina? This is the reason you can't go on that trip with the mystery guy?"

"Yeah, it is," I say as the blond woman moves on to some other news story.

"Well, if he watches Good Morning America, he already knows. They might have done the dirty work for you."

Terror races through my mind at the thought that Ian has just found out the truth I've been hiding for over a week from of all places a morning news show. "I have to go," I say frantically as I leap out of bed to get dressed. "I'll talk to you later, Sienna."

I don't give her a chance to answer before I click END and throw my phone on the bed. I run into the bathroom and see my messy hair in the mirror, but I don't have time to make myself even close to presentable. I need to get to Ian before this news ruins everything.

Dashing out the door, I remember I left my

phone on the bed so I race back and grab it only to see a text waiting for me. I take a deep breath and open my messages to see it's from Ian.

When were you going to tell me about Vancouver?

My heart sinks as I read the words. He saw the same thing Sienna and I saw. The sense of betrayal hangs off every word. Quickly, I text back a tepid excuse, but I know whatever I say can't change the fact that I lied.

I'm sorry. I didn't mean to lie.

My answer is pathetic. Whatever I meant to do, I kept my new film from him and now I've hurt the man I love for no reason other than my cowardice.

I want to explain to him, but I don't know what to say. I wait for him to text back, to tell me how disappointed he is in me, but he doesn't. His silence crushes me, so I finally try my best to explain why I did what I did. I have to try.

I wanted to tell you but then you were so excited about the Rome trip and I didn't want to disappoint you. I never meant to lie. I love you, Ian. Please call me.

I click SEND and wait for him to call, but after

five minutes I know he won't. His anger comes through loud and clear in the silence. Then he texts me and my worst fears are realized.

Without trust, we have nothing, Kristina.

He won't let me convince him to forgive me through texts, so I run out of my apartment and down the stairs to the sidewalk, half expecting him to be there waiting for me. But that can't happen today because I've hurt him.

As I run the blocks toward his apartment, I think about all the love he's shown me and I feel like the guilt is going to crush me. I have to see him to tell him I'm sorry and I'll do anything to make this up to him. We can go to Rome together as soon as I finish working on Original Sin. It won't be forever. I'll only be gone for a few months.

His building's doorman is a friendly face waiting to open the door to the lobby. Rushing past him, I hurry to catch the elevator, frantically pressing the button to get to his floor and wishing for once the elevator wasn't so slow. It's the longest minute of my life, and when the elevator doors open, I lurch out into his hallway on unsteady legs, weak from the feeling of sickness in my stomach.

Even before I knock on his door, I know he's

not there. I feel a sense of missing him already. But I knock anyway, a futile effort that makes me feel like I have some control over getting him back.

I don't, though.

No one answers my knocking and somewhere deep inside I worry he's gone. Gone from here, gone from New York, gone from my life. I begin to unravel, desperate to tell him my side of the story. If only I could explain myself, if only he could see how devastated I am that what I've done has ruined what we had.

I don't know where to go to find him, so I walk the streets back to my place as I text him over and over, but he never replies. Hour after hour passes, but if he's getting my messages he's not responding. Finally, I cry myself to sleep after I send him one last text and pray he'll finally answer me.

I love you, Ian. Please tell me you still love me too. Tell me it's not too late for me to fix this.

After tossing and turning for hours, I wake up determined to repair the damage I've done. I know I can if he'll just give me a chance. I pack my bags for our trip to Rome, knowing that if I don't show up on the set for the beginning of shooting, my career might suffer but I don't care about that. All I care about is getting Ian back.

I have the cab take me to his apartment, sure that he'll be there because our flight doesn't leave for four hours. Standing in front of his door with my suitcase, I knock and listen to hear him inside as he comes to let me in. I rehearsed what I plan to say on my way here. Now all I need is the chance to show him how much I love him.

As I wait for him to answer the door, I see an envelope sticking out from underneath it. Bending down, I pick it up and see it's addressed to me. My heart slams against my chest as my hands begin to shake. I don't want to read it, but I open it anyway and see the words that break my heart.

> *Kristina,*
>
> *Every time I asked you if you had something to tell me, you lied. Was everything we were a lie? I've gone to Rome. Don't try to contact me.*
>
> *Ian*

The tears roll down my cheeks as I read his words so filled with the pain I caused. I can't let him leave without me. I have to do this, even if it means ruining everything I've worked for in my career. I send him one more text to let him know I'm not giving up on us as I race downstairs to catch a cab to the airport.

I won't let you go without a fight. I'm coming to you.

CHAPTER NINE

Ian

I SIT IN the airport lounge waiting to board my plane and reading Kristina's texts after she found my letter I left her. I won't lie. Knowing this bothers her gives me at least some modicum of pleasure after feeling like I'd been kicked in the fucking stomach as I watched that morning show. Nothing like finding out the woman you love has been lying to you for days, even after you gave her more than enough chances to come clean.

Not that I can't forgive her. I can. I don't have a choice, to be honest. I love her too much to even think I can go on without her.

My phone vibrates against my glass of scotch, and I see it's Kristina. My eyes scan her text and I smile.

Don't give up on us. Please.

My instinct is to message her back and tell her I couldn't give up on what she is to me any more than I could give up breathing. Avoiding her for the last day has been pure torture. My hands yearn to touch her. I crave the feel of her skin on mine, the taste of her lips as she kisses me when I slide my cock into her and bury myself inside her body. My body aches from not having her next to me. I miss her smile, her voice, her laughter.

I miss her. And even though I'm hurt she lied, I just want her back with me so we can go to Rome and fall in love all over again.

I grab my phone and text back to her.

I can't give you up. Come to me.

Immediately, she answers my text with one of her own filled with that need so familiar in my life.

Promise you'll wait for me. Don't leave me here without you.

Texting back, I tell her what I know she wants to hear.

Meet me at Gate B 39. I left your ticket at the Delta desk. I love you.

I sit there as people come and go on their way to wherever they're going and wonder how many of them are like Kristina and me. Most people sleepwalk through life. They pretend to love, pretend to care about those around them. They fake it, phone in love and lust and all the things in life that make it worth living. People float in and out of their lives with little more than a nod in recognition.

But not us. Since the moment I met her, every part of me has felt alive like never before. With the first touch of my hand, she's been mine. When I see her after she's been gone for mere hours, it's like my eyes can't open wide enough to take in all of her. I want to touch her, feel her breath as I take it away with a kiss on her gorgeous lips or the perfect word whispered in her ear.

I finish my scotch and look at the time. One hour until boarding. Looking down at my phone, I begin to worry she won't make it before we have to leave. For the first time since I sat there in my apartment watching that insipid morning news show discuss how the woman I love had lied to me, the thought occurs to me that Kristina might truly choose something over me.

My stomach knots from the betrayal this thought brings with it. How could she? I'd never choose anyone or anything over her. I can't. She's as necessary to me as the food I eat and the air I breathe. It's never a choice to need her.

Something in leaving to go somewhere else

fills me with dread. When she left that night after I'd frightened her, I never doubted I'd see her again. Never doubted we'd be together again. Now as I sit in this lounge watching planes take off to faraway places, a niggling feeling gnaws at me that if she doesn't come to Rome with me, it's over.

We're over.

A little voice inside me asks the obvious question. How could that be? I'm no less addicted to her than I was to heroin, even more. Heroin only made me feel good and helped me forget what terrified me. Kristina gives me what no drug ever could.

Love in return. And that love makes me a better man. No drug has ever done that for me.

So how could this be the end of us? Am I not addicted to how incredible she makes me feel anymore?

Closing my eyes, I silently pray she shows up and I don't have to answer any of these questions. I don't want to think of life without her.

I wait until I can't anymore and slowly walk to the gate. My hands sweat and my legs feel weak. Looking up, I see the sign for Gate B 39 and stop to look around. People file past me as the flight attendants begin to call for first class boarding. I should get on the plane, but I can't.

Not without Kristina. She's coming. I just need to wait a little longer.

First class finishes boarding and I'm still standing in line. The petite brunette flight attendant gives me a confused look as if to ask, "Are you coming?"

I flash her a weak smile and step back out of line as she announces that coach class can now begin boarding. More people file past me into the tube that leads to the plane as I search left and right for Kristina.

My phone vibrates and I know even before I look that I don't want to read the message. I can't avoid it, though, so I bring it up on the screen and see everything I've dreaded since yesterday.

I tried to get there but I can't.

There's more, but I can't read it. Stuffing my phone back into my pocket, I get into line and make my way to the flight attendant. She gives me a sad look like she knows I've just spent the last fifteen minutes waiting for someone who was never going to show. Giving me a tepid smile, she wishes me a good flight and sends me down the tube to board the plane alone.

A few minutes later, I'm settled into my seat and look over at the empty seat next to me, my chest tightening as the reality sinks in. Kristina chose something over us.

Over me.

I look at my phone as everyone around me tells the attendant their drink orders and feel too sick to my stomach to even try to down any more alcohol. Her message sits there on my phone staring up at me. Dismissing me.

My publicist caught me as I tried to go to you and stopped me. I want to be there with you, but I can't give up the chance this film offers me. Please forgive me.

My fingers don't move to text back. I have nothing to say.

Please answer me. Say something. Anything. Please! Tell me we're going to be okay. Tell me you forgive me. Please Ian.

The plane's engines roar and we begin to taxi down the runway as I finally answer her message with one last text of my own.

Goodbye

As I turn my phone off, she texts again telling me she won't let me go and that she loves me, but I don't have anything else to say. The plane takes off into the air above Kennedy, and for me I'm not going to Rome so much as leaving her.

Leaving everything we were, including our

story, behind. Whatever we had she ruined by lying to me.

Halfway over the Atlantic, I read over her messages again and see one that came in after I turned off my phone. Full of the sadness I feel, it shows the strength I love in her, and I silently pray she means what she wrote.

You said there was no running from what we are, Ian. I can't let this be goodbye. You can't either. We will see each other again.

IAN AND KRISTINA'S STORY CONTINUES IN SHATTER (ADDICTED TO YOU #3) GET YOUR COPY TODAY!

IF I DREAM (CORRUPTED LOVE #1)

A story of passion, crime, and the lengths you go to for love…

If I dream, will you dare?

Ryder
All I wanted was my freedom. It's all I'd dreamed of from the first time I stood in the ring. Until I entered Robert Erickson's world. Until Serena. Cruelty and ugliness surrounded me, but she was beautiful and good. I wanted to protect her from her father's world, even though I knew being with her could mean the end of me.

Serena
I wanted for nothing as the daughter of one of the richest men in the world. But all my father's money couldn't buy what I truly craved. Until Ryder. I wanted all he was, all he brought out in me. All he made me desire.

Our love was forbidden by the one person who had the power to harm us. We dreamed of more than living in that world, though. We dreamed of having it all, but did we dare?

CHAPTER ONE

Ryder

A S USUAL, THE crowd at The Pit screamed its lust for the two of us to pound the fuck out of each other. Impatient bastards. I couldn't hear any one person's words clearly, but I'd done this enough times to know what the people who'd come to watch us wanted.

Blood. Pain. And one of us as close to death as possible. It thrilled them in some sick way almost as much as I suspected winning did when their fighter crushed another person.

My opponent tonight stood nearly as tall as I did at six foot three, but his body was smaller than mine. He looked older, like something in the way he carried himself said he'd seen more of life than I had. His angular face looked hard, and on either side of his perfectly straight nose were eyes staring me down like he thought squinting and grimacing would make me run for the nearest exit like some fucking scared little boy. He was fighting the wrong person if that's what he expected.

I'd never lost and for good reason. When you had nothing but the feel of your fists beating the hell out of someone and the sound of those rabid fucks cheering you on like you were some kind of hero for nearly killing another man, all you wanted was to win.

Fifteen times I'd won right here in this dank warehouse against guys bigger and stronger than me, and every time it seemed to surprise everyone. Even those who had bet on me.

If they only knew how unlikely it was anyone could match the rage inside me, they'd never bet against me again.

Some impatient bastard behind me barked, "Stop dancing around! Hit 'em!"

Mr. Grimace narrowed his eyes until he could barely see out of them and took a deep breath. Why did he bother with all this tough guy bullshit? That's not what these bloodthirsty fucks wanted.

Pain is what they wanted.

So that's what they'd get. His or mine. It didn't matter to them.

"Scared, motherfucker?" he grunted out in a deep voice I knew wasn't really how he talked. "I'm going to fuck you up."

I didn't bother answering.

He caught me in the face with a hard right that scrambled my brains for a second, and then his fist skidded along my jaw and ran square into my right shoulder. The last guy I fought had done a number on that one, so that hurt like a bitch.

I knew how this went, though. The people around us wanted a show as much as they wanted a fight. I could have just beat the fuck out of him and won, but that's not what this was. I'd been told that enough times to understand even if I could pound the piss out of a guy, I had to at least make it look like a fight and not just some sad beat down.

So that's what I did. I took a few hits, sometimes more than a few, and let it look like there was some chance I wouldn't win. The other guy got to feel pretty big in the shorts and the crowd got to feel like this was really a match between two fighters.

It wasn't, though.

He paraded around like a peacock, preening to the crowd while I gritted my teeth and pushed my shoulder back into place. I took a deep breath and waited for the moment I'd show him who he was dealing with.

Flush with the love of the crowd, he turned back to face me. A few shots into me had made him think he had a chance.

I stepped forward as he lunged at me and leveled my fist against his jaw. His head ricocheted back, sending him reeling for a second or two, but I didn't let up. My right hand zeroed in on his face again, this time connecting with his cheekbone. I felt it crack against my knuckles bulging out of my fist and saw him stagger back away from me.

But he would get no mercy from me. That wasn't what I was here for.

"Get him!" the crowd screamed as the guy cowered, hanging his head to protect his busted face.

That wouldn't help him, though. Not with me. I knew what my role was. I knew why all these people had come here tonight, and it wasn't to see mercy. Mercy was for suckers. Fuck mercy.

They wanted blood and pain, and blood and pain is what they'd get.

I walked toward him as a feeling of complete calm came over me. All the noise of the crowd around us faded away until all I heard were the words I told myself every time I stood to fight.

It's you or him. Nothing more. Either you win or he does, but if you lose, you'll have nothing.

He looked up and I saw the pleading in his eyes. I'd seen it fifteen times before. No matter how big and tough they'd been in the beginning, each one ended up giving me that same sad look that said they wanted me to be someone other than who they'd heard I was.

Someone other than who I had to be.

Maybe they fought for some reason that had nothing to do with their very survival. Maybe they thought it would be fun, or it would make them feel tough. Maybe they thought they had something to prove to some girl. Whatever their reasons for agreeing to fight, they weren't why I fought.

For me, every win put me one step closer to being free. I didn't fight for shits and giggles or because I wanted to impress some skirt. I fought for the chance that one day I would never have to step foot in this fucking shithole place again. I fought because deep in the back of my mind there existed the tiniest dream that one day I'd be normal and have a normal life.

That one day I wouldn't have to be the man I'd been forced to become in this fight.

I knew his weak spots and attacked them. My fists pummeled his face, and no matter how hard he tried to shield himself from the blows, it was no use. Over and over, I hit him until that pretty face of his looked like mangled hamburger. Blood, flesh, and bone mixed to make a horror show. The nose that had been so straight just a few minutes before now pointed down toward his mouth like some deranged compass.

As I stood up to my full height, I heard the crowd cheering, as if I'd done something worthy of praise. A man lay in a crumpled heap at my feet, defeated and broken, and these fuckers were thrilled about it.

Looking around, I saw some clapping and others pumping their fists in the air as my win filled them with some kind of messed up happiness. Who was I kidding? What it filled was their wallets. That's why they were so happy.

Floyd raised my right arm in the air to the delight of the rabid fans and said in my ear, "That's my boy. You done good, son."

I forced a smile and nodded my head. I wasn't his boy and he wasn't my father. I was his fighter and he was the scumbag who went out to find people for me to fight. Whatever else he thought we were was all in his mind.

He lowered my arm and slapped me on the back. "Go relax. You deserve it. You put on a good show. Just look at the way these people love you!"

I tore my stare from his greasy comb-over and beady eyes and looked over his head to see the people who loved me. Between the booze, the drugs, and the fight, they looked like wild animals.

Who was worse? Them or me?

"RYDER, THERE'S SOMEONE here to talk to you," Floyd yelled from the other side of the door.

I didn't want to talk to anyone. All I wanted to do was sit on my crappy metal folding chair in this dingy room and hope my shoulder started feeling better. I'd downed a few shots of Floyd's whisky about ten minutes ago, but so far, it hadn't helped ease the pain.

"Not now," I yelled back.

He'd only open the door anyway. I knew that. It still felt good to let him and whoever the hell was standing there with him know that I didn't want to talk.

The door opened a second later and I saw Floyd and some guy who looked far too well-dressed to be anywhere near the warehouse on any night standing in my shitty little room. He had a vibe that screamed money with his suit, expensive shoes, and slicked back grey hair that made him look what my mother used to call stately.

"This is Mr. Robert Erickson," Floyd said as the man walked into the room like he owned the place. "I'll leave you two to talk."

I'd never seen Floyd leave a scene that fast. As he closed the door, I looked at the man who stood in front of me and saw he was studying me as much as I was him. Not that I was all too curious about what he wanted. People dressed like he was coming into my world never brought anything good with them.

Never.

The intruder looked around the cinder block room I called mine and then looked down at me. "Ryder, as our mutual friend Floyd said, my name is Robert Erickson. Do you know who I am?"

Shaking my head, I shrugged. "Nope. Should I?"

His dark eyebrows drew in like angry black slashes and his eyes narrowed to slits, much like the way the guy I just beat to a pulp had looked at the beginning of our fight. "I'm the man who runs this show. You are sitting in my warehouse and fighting in my stable. So yes, maybe you should know who I am."

As much as I knew he thought I should be impressed by this, I wasn't. Folding my arms across my chest, I said, "Oh yeah? Nice to meet the big boss then. I hope you bet on me tonight."

His eyes opened wider as the corners of his mouth inched up into what reminded me of how a crocodile looked right before he ate his prey. "You're pretty sure of yourself, aren't you?"

I looked up at the ceiling for a moment,

unsure how I should answer that. Fuck yeah, I was sure of myself. I may not have been wearing a thousand dollar suit and fine leather shoes like him, but I had gifts of my own that had made me a winner sixteen times already.

Pursing my lips, I shrugged again. "I haven't lost yet. Come see me when I do and I'll tell you how cocky I'm feeling then."

His crocodile smile spread even wider across his face. Nodding, he said, "I'll remember that. For now, I'm here to tell you I've bought your contract from Floyd. So now you work for only me."

The words hit me like a fist to the face. I didn't have a contract with Floyd or anyone else. I fought to pay off money I owed him, and when that debt was paid off, I'd get to leave this shithole world of fighting. Now all that seemed like a pipe dream this fucker had dashed to pieces.

I stood from my rusted metal chair and stared at Robert Erickson. "What does that mean?"

Nearly the same height, he met my gaze with one so intense I thought about taking a step back. When he spoke, it sounded like his voice came from somewhere dark.

"It means I own you now. You fight for me and I expect you to win like you always have."

Left unsaid was the implicit threat that hung

off every word. If you lose, you'll suffer. The only question was how.

My mind spun at the news that all I'd planned, all I'd worked for, was gone now. "So I guess my deal with Floyd to be released from fighting when I paid off what I owed him is gone too?"

"Yes."

"And if I don't agree to this new deal?" I asked, silently gauging my chances of not only getting past him but finding some way of surviving after I got away. He was big, and I had a sneaking suspicion even bigger guys stood outside waiting for him.

Robert Erickson looked like the type of man who got what he wanted, one way or another, whether the other person involved wanted it or not.

"You have no say in it, but let me assure you that you want to fight for me. For now, let's get you to your place so you can pack your things."

He turned to open the door as I explained this room was my place. "No need to go anywhere. You're already in it."

Erickson slowly looked back at me with confusion written all over his face. "You live here?"

I nodded. "Yeah. Short commute time to

work and everything I need within arm's reach. What more could a guy ask for?"

Closing the door, he turned to face me. "How old are you?"

"Eighteen."

"And you live here, in my warehouse where Floyd holds fights for me?" he asked as he looked around my room again, this time with a look of disgust like the fact made him sick.

"Yep. Better than the street or jail. I might not get three hots, but I got a cot and a shower."

My answer didn't make the sickened expression leave his face, but he nodded anyway. "Well, gather your things. It's time to go."

I opened my mouth to ask where, but he walked out and left me standing there in that room I'd lived in for the past three months. As I stuffed the few clothes I owned, deodorant, and my toothbrush into a duffel bag, I thought wherever I was going had to be better than this place.

WE PULLED UP to a massive black gate between two even bigger rows of hedges and stopped momentarily as the driver got the go ahead to drive onto the property. I couldn't help but stare out the window as we drove up the long driveway past some kind of fountain that looked like something the Greek gods might swim in and a bunch of smaller hedges than the ones out front that looked like the gardener had cut them all into bird shapes. Robert Erickson was even richer than I'd first thought. Only insanely wealthy people lived in places like this.

The car stopped in front of a house so big I couldn't see all of it as I looked out the car window. Erickson tapped me on the arm as I stared out at the mansion and said, "Welcome home."

Home? This couldn't be my home. Instantly, the thought of what I'd have to do to live in a place like this raced through my mind. Fighting in The Pit wasn't going to be enough to live in a house like the one I saw in front of me.

I opened the car door and stepped out onto a stone driveway as I gaped at the house, which was even more impressive without the tinting of the car window getting in my way. Huge white columns towered above us to the second story of the gold colored home, and a glass front door so enormous I'd never seen one so big stood behind them.

"Follow me," was all Erickson said as he led the way to those doors. I couldn't imagine what waited inside after an outside this incredible.

I did as he ordered and caught up to him as he

walked into an entryway so big the sound of our shoes hitting the white marble tile on the floor echoed off the matching marble tiled walls. He strode through like nothing around us was special toward the most spectacular curved wrought iron staircase I'd ever seen.

Not that I had seen many curved staircases with wrought iron in my life. I think I'd seen either a grand total of two times in a magazine some girl had in English class one time. I really didn't have much interest in reading architectural magazines, but she did and since I wanted to get in her pants, I sat next to her after school as she told me all about her dreams of having a huge house with a curved staircase and a wrought iron railing one day.

She would have loved Erickson's place. For me, it made me feel small, something very few people or things had achieved in a long time. Not small, actually. More like insignificant.

As my head swiveled left and right to look at the artwork on the walls, Robert said, "Come in here to my office. I want you to meet some people."

My hand clutched the handle of my duffel bag tightly in my palm. Meet some people? I didn't even look like they'd let me on the property to be the goddamned gardener who made hedges into animal shapes and now he wanted to introduce me to some people?

That feeling of insignificance morphed into one of pure discomfort. I didn't belong there, no matter how much he wanted to parade me through the place, and whoever he wanted me to meet would know that as sure as I did.

He led me into his office, a room even bigger than the entryway and as dark as that was light. This room had dark green walls the color of a pool table and a dark wood floor. Floor to ceiling bookcases held books with names I'd never heard of and sculptures I guessed cost more than my life was worth.

"Wait here. I'll be right back," he announced before leaving as I continued to look around in awe.

Seconds later, he came back with two females and ordered them into his office. Neither one looked like him, but something about the way they acted told me they weren't servants or people he'd just basically bought, like me.

They stopped dead at the sight of me standing there in my old gym pants and black t-shirt and the one I figured was older spun around to look at him in disgust.

"Who is this?"

"Girls, this is Ryder. He's going to be living

here, so treat him like family."

Robert's proclamation infuriated her, and she shook her head angrily. "What, like a brother? You go out one night and get us a brother? Is that how it goes, Dad?"

He ignored her outburst and turned his two daughters to face me. "Ryder, the one who can't stop talking is Janelle. The other one is Serena."

"Hi," I mumbled, unsure if I should say anything.

They both stood staring at me like I was some foreign thing that needed to be removed and fast. The one named Janelle had short dark brown hair, and although I couldn't be sure since her eyes were flashing so much hatred, I thought they were brown too. Thin, she wore jeans and a tight blue shirt and heels that gave her at least three inches on her normal height.

The other one, Serena, had lighter brown hair that fell to below her shoulders in soft waves that reminded me of what mermaids looked like. Dressed in jean shorts and a white t-shirt that both showed off her tan and toned body, she stood barefoot next to her father and stared at me with big brown eyes that didn't have hatred but something else in them.

Disappointment?

As Janelle returned to complaining about my

very existence, I heard Serena say in a pained voice, "You said you knew where she was. You promised you'd find her this time. Where is she?"

I imagined that's what that guy with the pleading eyes would have sounded like if he begged me not to beat the shit out of him. The way she said those words made my chest hurt, and I didn't even know who she was talking about.

But Robert was unmoved by her pleading. Waving off her questions, he said, "Maybe next time, honey. For now, I want you two to welcome Ryder to our home."

He put his arms around both of them, but Janelle slipped out of his hold and stormed off without another word. I didn't have to guess how she felt about me. Serena said nothing more about what was obviously so important to her and simply looked at me with that pleading in her eyes that hadn't worked on her father.

With a nudge from him, she finally said, "Welcome to our home. I hope you like it here."

And with that, she quietly left without another word to her father about whoever she wanted him to find.

Robert walked behind his desk and sat down in his chair as I watched her walk away, her sagging shoulders signaling how defeated she felt. Clearly, it didn't affect her father at all.

"They'll get used to you. Janelle is a little temperamental, but I guess that's to be expected from a girl, even one her age. She's a lot like me, though, so at least she has that going for her. Serena is the polar opposite. She's like her mother. Don't worry about her. She'll take to you like every stray she brings home."

Not that I didn't know I looked like some stray dog compared to them, but the way he said it brought the reality home for sure. In a hurry to get out of there and to wherever he kept the strays he brought home, I said, "Well, if you can just point me in the direction of where you want me to go, I'll get out of your hair."

He shook his head as that crocodile smile spread across his face again. "Not yet. First, I want you to know what I expect of you. So sit down and relax."

Dropping my duffel bag, I sat down in a chair in front of his desk as he'd ordered and listened to hear just what this whole arrangement would involve.

He steepled his fingers in front of him and began. "You'll continue to fight as you did tonight. As I said before, I expect you to continue to win. When you do, you'll get paid, despite the fact that you won't need money as long as you live here."

"I won't need money?" I asked, confused what kind of world this guy lived in that didn't require cash.

Lifting his chin, he shook his head. "No, you won't. Your room and board, along with all the food you want and clothes you need, will be provided. I have a state of the art workout center you're to use to make sure you're in the best shape possible. So you see, you won't need money."

I didn't know if I should question this whole situation that sounded too good to be true, but I asked, "And if I don't win a fight?"

His face grew dark. "Let's cross that bridge when we come to it. For now, I have very few rules, other than you performing in fights like I've seen. No drugs and no romantic attachments. I don't care who you fuck, but don't get involved. I remember being your age, so I don't expect you to live like a monk, but no relationships."

I wasn't a fan of having so much of my life dictated, but assuming I got a room even as big as a broom closet on his estate, maybe it wouldn't be too much of a tradeoff. I wasn't exactly looking for a relationship anyway and I didn't do drugs. Hoping he wasn't about to announce that I had to double as a stable boy or something like that, I smiled.

"Okay. I can live with those."

"And you aren't to tell anyone here what you do. Is that clear?"

"Sure. But if I'm not here as a fighter, what am I supposed to say if someone asks?"

"They won't," he said with a confidence I guessed came from being the boss.

"Got it."

"Good. I'll have my housekeeper take you to your room. For now, you'll have the spare bedroom on this floor."

A short, dark haired woman he called Josephine appeared a few seconds later, so I stood from my chair and grabbed my duffel bag to go with her. I felt like there were a lot more questions I should ask Robert, but he didn't seem interested in talking anymore and picked up the phone to call someone, so I smiled again and moved to leave.

Just before I reached the door, he said, "Oh, Ryder, one more thing."

There it was. The one thing that would make this whole situation unbearable. I slowly turned around and waited for the other shoe to drop.

"Don't even think of doing anything with either of the girls. In that respect, I do care who you fuck."

I thought back to how much Janelle hated me already and easily put the idea of fucking her out of my mind. And Serena? I wasn't sure if she was even legal, and I didn't need that dogging me. An angry father was one thing, but prison was an entirely different story.

She was beautiful, though. There was something about her I could definitely like, if things were different. But no matter how beautiful she was, I wasn't touching that.

"No problem," I answered with confidence, hoping that was the worst thing about living at Erickson's house.

If it was, this would be the best thing to ever happen to me, even if it meant I had to keep fighting. Maybe freedom wasn't all it was cracked up to be anyway.

**LOOK FOR THE CORRUPTED LOVE
TRILOGY TODAY!
AVAILABLE AT ALL MAJOR RETAILERS**

About the Author

K.M. Scott writes contemporary romance stories of sexy, intense, and unforgettable love. A New York Times and USA Today bestselling author, she's been in love with romance since reading her first romance novel in junior high (she was a very curious girl!). Under her Gabrielle Bisset name, she writes erotic paranormal and historical romance. She lives in Pennsylvania with a herd of animals and when she's not writing can be found reading or feeding her TV addiction.

Be sure to visit K.M.'s Facebook page at **facebook.com/kmscottauthor** for all the latest on her books, along with giveaways and other goodies! And to hear all the news on K.M. Scott books first, sign up for her newsletter today and be sure to visit her website at **www.kmscottbooks.com**.

Books by K.M. Scott:

If I Dream (Corrupted Love #1)
If You Fight (Corrupted Love #2)
If We Fall (Corrupted Love #3)

Crash Into Me (Heart of Stone #1)
Fall Into Me (Heart of Stone #2)
Give In To Me (Heart of Stone #3)
Heart of Stone Volume One Box Set
Ever After (Heart of Stone #4)
A Heart of Stone Christmas (Heart of Stone #5)
Unforgettable (Heart of Stone #6)
Unbreakable (Heart of Stone #7)
Heart of Stone Volume Two Box Set

Temptation (Club X #1)
Surrender (Club X #2)
Possession (Club X #3)
Satisfaction (Club X #4)
Acceptance (Club X #5)
The Complete Club X Series Box Set

Crave (Addicted To You #1)
Adore (Addicted To You #2)
Shatter (Addicted To You #3)
Claim (Addicted To You #4)

K.M.'S BOOKS ARE IN AUDIOBOOK TOO!

Books by Gabrielle Bisset:

Vampire Dreams Revamped (A Sons of Navarus Prequel)
Blood Avenged (Sons of Navarus #1)
Blood Betrayed (Sons of Navarus #2)
Longing (A Sons of Navarus Short Story)
Blood Spirit (Sons of Navarus #3)
The Deepest Cut (A Sons of Navarus Short Story)
Blood Prophecy (Sons of Navarus #4)
Blood Craving (Sons of Navarus #5)
Blood Eclipse (Sons of Navarus #6)
The Sons of Navarus Box Set #1
The Sons of Navarus Box Set #2

Stolen Destiny (Destined Ones Duology #1)
Destiny Redeemed (Destined Ones Duology #2)

Love's Master
Masquerade
The Victorian Erotic Romance Trilogy